MADISON SMARTT BELL

The Color of Night

Madison Smartt Bell is the author of fifteen previous
works of fiction, including *All Souls' Rising* (a National
Book Award finalist), *Soldier's Joy,* and *Anything Goes.* He
lives in Baltimore, Maryland, where he teaches in the
Creative Writing Program at Goucher College.

http://faculty.goucher.edu/mbell/

Also by Madison Smartt Bell

The Washington Square Ensemble
Waiting for the End of the World
Straight Cut
Zero db
The Year of Silence
Soldier's Joy
Barking Man
Doctor Sleep
Save Me, Joe Louis
All Souls' Rising
Ten Indians
Narrative Design: A Writer's Guide to Structure
Master of the Crossroads
Anything Goes
The Stone That the Builder Refused
*Lavoisier in the Year One: The Birth of a New Science
    in an Age of Revolution*
Toussaint Louverture: A Biography
Charm City: A Walk Through Baltimore
Devil's Dream

THE
COLOR
OF
NIGHT

THE
COLOR
OF
NIGHT

Madison Smartt Bell

VINTAGE BOOKS

A Division of Random House, Inc.

New York

A VINTAGE BOOKS ORIGINAL, APRIL 2011

Copyright © 2011 by Madison Smartt Bell

All rights reserved. Published in the United States by Vintage Books,
a division of Random House, Inc., New York, and in Canada by Random
House of Canada Limited, Toronto.

Vintage and colophon are registered trademarks of Random House, Inc.

Library of Congress Cataloging-in-Publication Data
Bell, Madison Smartt.
The color of night : a novel / by Madison Smartt Bell.
p. cm.
ISBN 978-0-307-74188-2
1. Card dealers—Fiction.   2. Las Vegas (Nev.)—Fiction.   3. Marginality,
Social—Fiction.   4. Social isolation—Fiction.   5. Psychological fiction.
I. Title.
PS3552.E517C65 2011
813'.54—dc21
2010019104

Book design by Ralph Fowler

www.vintagebooks.com

Printed in the United States of America
10 9 8 7 6 5 4 3 2 1

Pou mystè ki te mande'm fè'l

I have always said that my work is dictated to me by daemons. People probably think that's a figure of speech; maybe this book will prove it literal. Surely it is the most vicious and appalling story ever to pass through my hand to the page, so inevitably some people will hate it. I thank Jane Gelfman, Marie-Catherine Vacher, and Deborah Schneider for believing in its value when no one else did; Edward Kastenmeier, Sonny Mehta, and Diana Coglianese for the catalytic roles they played; and (especially) Dan Frank, for seeing in a different light.

This book was completed with support from the Harold and Mildred Strauss Living awarded by the American Academy of Arts and Letters.

Forgive is too weak a word. Recall the idea of
Até, which was so real to the Greeks. Até is the
name of the almost automatic transfer of suffering
from one being to another. Power is a form of Até.
The victims of power, and any power has its
victims, are themselves infected. They have
then to pass it on, to use the power on others.

—IRIS MURDOCH, *The Unicorn*

THE
COLOR
OF
NIGHT

1

Until the day the towers fell, I'd long believed that all the gods were dead. For years, for decades, my head was still. Only sometimes, deep in the desert, the soughing ghost voice of O———. But still, the bell of my head was silent, swinging aimlessly over the void.

* * *

I could watch it again, as much as I wanted, since the TV kept playing it over and over like a game of Tetris no one could win. No limit to how many times I could consume, could devour those images. Again and again the rapid swelling, ripening to the bursting point, and then the fall. The buckling, crumbling, blooming outward in that great orb of ruin before it showered all its matter to the ground. Those gnatlike specks that swirled around it proved to be mortals, springing out of the flames. Wrapped in the shrouds of their screaming, they sailed down.

It didn't matter how many saw one watching, since none can know another's heart or mind. I had not known my blood could rise like that. Still, again, despite the years, the withering of my body.

Sometimes the television showed a plane biting into the side of a building, its teeth on its underside where the mouth of a shark is—then flame leaped up from the wound like the red surge from an artery. Then there were shots of living mortals on the street, wailing, raking the flesh from the bone of their faces, or some of them frozen, prostrate with awe.

So I saw Laurel for the first time again, Laurel kneeling on the sidewalk, her head thrown back, her hands stretched out with the fingers crooked, as weapons or in praise. Blood was running from the corners of her mouth, like in the old days, though not for the same reason.

2

Inside the casino, it never happened. Nothing there can enter in. Only the whirl of lights and the electronic burbling of machines, rattle of dice in the craps table cups, an almost inaudible whisper of cards, the friction-free hum of roulette wheels turning. Nothing is permitted to change.

It is a sort of fifth-rate hell, and I a minor demon posted to it. A succubus too indifferent to suck. I have my regulars, of course. Sometimes I even know their names. I deal them cards and they lose money. Occasionally one of them wins, of course, but not for long.

"Mae," tonight's mark says. My name's a little sinister in his faint Slavic accent. He's told me his but I've forgotten. A retired airline pilot, I think he said. Some would find him good-looking, in that square-headed way all the pilots have. Silver hair and a face burnt to wrinkly leather. It takes a long time to catch a buzz from the watered drinks they give free here, but my regular has the determination to do it.

"When you get off work, Mae? When you coming home with me?" I part my painted lips to show my pleasant teeth to him, smooth away the black wing of my hair. I am conscious of not looking up at the dark bulb in the low tiled ceiling, where the two of us are captured by a fish-eye lens. I am older than he, perhaps a lot older, but as far as I know he doesn't know it.

I show my hole card: eight to a jack. Not much of a hand, but my regular took a hit too many and he's busted.

I might have worked a double shift, meaning sixteen hours straight. Sometimes I do. I don't get tired. Even in a fifth-rate hell there is no sense of the passage of time. I don't remember anything unusual that day—if there were fewer people than we normally got, a sudden emptying of the place, illumination from outside. No, I don't think there was that. It hardly matters what I recall, since no one is going to call me to witness, at least not on that point.

Probably two hours of darkness remained by the time I got into my car. It takes barely a quarter of that to drive from the casino to my dwelling. I don't listen to radio. I don't like the chatter, and I don't like music with singing in it, and I don't like to hear guitars or strings. Maybe I listened to piano during the dark drive, Bach or Chopin, in a minor key. No voice told me what rent had been torn in the world that day. When I went into the desert, I still didn't know.

3

The trailer park was shut up tight with chain-link fence, but I had broken some of the links with a bolt cutter, right behind my tiny deck, so I could walk directly into the desert when I pleased. When I went through I pressed my palm against the jagged ends of the cut wire, not quite hard enough to break the skin, and then I pulled the pieces back together so the tear in the fence wouldn't be too obvious, in case anyone were to look, which no one would.

In one of the trailers behind me a television was muttering and in another an old woman wept, in harsh, ugly, choking sobs. I walked until these sounds disappeared, holding my back to the spangle of lights of the town behind. I could hear only my own rubber soles crunching on the pale dust of the desert, and that not much, for I walked very softly. Sometimes I took the rifle and didn't kill anything. Tonight I had left the rifle behind and I was empty-handed.

I crossed fat tracks of an ATV in the sand, and farther south the string of $S S S$ left by a sidewinder. No sign of the snake itself. The desert looked flat and empty as the moon. The moon, the real one, had not risen. Selene had not stepped into her car.

The stars were cold and far away and I stood under them with my knees slightly bent and my back to the desert wind, which rushed through my legs and the sleeves of my shirt and dragged my dark hair forward around my face. Ambient light from Las Vegas bled into the sky from the north and dimmed the stars. Rage. Rage. It grew and then faded.

The wind fell then and as it died a great owl stooped across my left shoulder, in a perfect silence that thrilled down my spine through the soles of my feet into the sand. As the owl struck silently, out of my sight, some rodent uttered a desperate shriek—piercing, but it didn't last long.

There. That would do. But I remained, still where I stood for a few minutes longer. I curled my fingers into my palm, feeling an edge of nail against the skin. I would need to cut my fingernails before tomorrow. I keep them short.

The stillness surrounding me was not quite perfect; I could still hear the drone of cars on a highway some-where, and maybe, on some distant ridge, white turbines of a wind farm. The wind returned, fitfully now, bring-ing a soughing sound as it dragged across some cavity, a set of lips, a hole. As sometimes happened, I seemed to hear O——'s voice singing in the space between the stars

. . . ταύρος—ταύρος—χορν'δ και thro "η κατάθλιφη της νύχτας. Με τα αστέρια που περιβάλλοναι, και με το φανό της ευρείας . . .

fitfully too, intermittent, senseless. Or I would not admit the sense

. . . ο του οποίου ηλέκτρινος σφαίρα κάνει το απεικ-ονισμένο μεσημέρι της νύχτας:

the longing, the eternal sadness, vexed me. The sonor-ity of his meaninglessness

. . . Εραστής των αλόγων, θαυμάσιος . . .

But of course it was only the wind after all. Or at least it stopped, before my heart turned completely black.

The wind switched direction, bringing grit into the corners of my eyes. I turned away from it, toward the vacant glitter of the town. Soon dawn would come. Fatigue was a gray square in my brain, between my eyes. I might almost be tired enough to sleep.

When I came back inside the trailer I cast about till I found my nail clippers, their cheap metal silver in the first thin light of the morning. I tore open a pack of jerky for breakfast, and without thinking about it I snapped on the television and there it all was. A hole in the world. Through the fissure of the TV screen it all came washing over me.

4

I don't know how to begin, because I have no desire to begin.

Again.

It's again . . .

5

The first time I ever saw Laurel, her head was thrown back, laughing. She had completely abandoned herself to that laugh, but I didn't know what was so funny since I had just walked in the door. Or D——— had just sort of pushed me in, I think, and then he vaporized somewhere. I'm sure there must have been incense burning, and a few other people sitting around on cushions or a couple of bench seats ripped out of cars and dropped bang onto the splintery floor. Laurel looked soft to me, at first, and juicy. She was wearing a ribbed tank top and I could see the areolae of her breasts through the thin cotton. I looked a little longer than I should have, wondering why I might be interested in that. Then her chin came down and her chestnut curls flounced around her face, and she was looking at me steadily, seriously, though little chimes of laughter still spilled from the corners of her mouth. Her eyes were green and flecked with gold.

"So you're it," she said, and swallowed a giggle. "You're the new thing." The titter overcame her. She was higher than an asteroid, naturally; they all were. Whatever she was on I wasn't, but I began to catch that chokey cedar smell, not quite covered by the incense smoke.

"The next new thing!" Laurel got up and whirled around with her hair flying loose and her plump little hands stretched out to show the room to me and me to the room. There were those other people there, disposable people, I'm not sure who, but certainly one or two of the other girls, and probably a couple of guys with the sunken chests and the Jesus hair . . . one with a silver ankh on a string of beads, hanging between the open panels of his vest. That would be Ned, I think Ned was probably there that first day.

Laurel sobered up and looked me in the eye again. "I'm sorry," she said. "It's just . . . you know!"

But I didn't know. I knew some things then, but I didn't know that. She took my hand. It felt very natural, like a little girl taking the hand of her friend, and there was something maternal in it too, I can see now, and the rest was Laurel, being stoned. She was comparing my edge to her softness and showing it to the random people in the room—I don't remember what they were doing, talking to each other or nodded out or looking at the two of us together. A 45 record was going around and around on a record player that opened up like a briefcase; it might have been one of O——'s early hits. The laughter bottled inside Laurel was making me start to smile, without meaning to, which was rare.

"Look at us," she said, a mad look dancing with the gold spots in her eyes. "You're the knife. And I'm the butter."

The laughter overflowed from her again. "Come on," she said. "Let's blow." She tugged me toward the back door of the room, onto the gangplank that ran along the other rooms of the crazy structure I had just entered. The room we'd left had begun with a school bus that had sort of sunk into the sand when its tires went flat, I suppose, and when they needed more space than the bus, they'd knocked out the panels from one side and framed a bigger room against it and tacked on a tin roof that overlapped the rusted yellow metal of the bus. The whole thing straggled on from there.

The gangplank had a tin roof too, and from under its eaves I could see away, away across the desert to the mountains on the horizon, turning a brilliant violet color as the sun began to sink into them. But Laurel was tugging me along to her room. There wasn't a door, just a bead curtain. We rattled through it. Another joss stick burned inside. More cushions and a double mattress on the floor, a little table with an oval mirror reflecting up. Instead of a roof on Laurel's room there was canvas stretched over the two-by-six A-frame, which made it feel like some nomad's tent.

On a wall was one of those throbbing op-art circles, and I had to look away from that right away so I wouldn't throw up or have a seizure. My eye caught on another poster, black-and-white: a pale, slender woman lying naked on her back, with her head turned to the right, looking somewhere away. The pool of her thighs was filled with jewels; a vagina dentata with diamonds for teeth. Of course that's not the way I saw it then. The caption was the sort of thing that passed for insight in those days: *The jewelry is worth such-and-such. The rest is priceless.*

The room had filled up with sunset light, and above us the canvas sighed with the breeze. Laurel had let go of my hand, though she still stood close, appraising me. There was a touch of red in her hair, I saw now, and she had a scatter of cinnamon freckles over her cheekbones, and a pleasant scent of musk and light sweat. I began to feel the reef under her fluid surface. Her eyes were taking my measure now. Of course she had to be balling D——— too—we all did that, if we liked it or not. In his theory there was no such thing as jealousy but in practice he used it as a sword.

"Mae," Laurel said, tasting my name with the tip of her tongue. I was sure I hadn't told her my name. I had not yet addressed her one word.

"You can stay here, Mae," she said. "With me."

6

The town where I now lived had been made for the people who built Hoover Dam, and for a long time there was no gambling there, because the workers didn't want it, or because the powers that then were didn't want them to have it. The nearest casino was to be found in a slash through the mountains just to the north, first cut for the railroad to go through. It always looked calm from the outside, at evening especially, a great sand-colored rectangle, nothing but functional, but with clean square lines that gave it, sometimes, the aspect of a temple. A wide range of stone steps spilled down from the entrance, a recession of squares outlined in tubes of red and blue neon. The lights around the doorway didn't flash. On September 12, I entered at dusk.

Business as usual. My table was three-quarters full for most of the night. A few regulars, and a few strays, as usual. It's possible they talked more among themselves than they normally did, exchanging horror stories and conspiracy theories. I don't know; I never listened to what the mortals said to one another. It meant less than birdsong to me.

There was one I had never seen before, an Indian, or he looked like one. He was big and broad, with blunt features softening with age, with alcohol too, more than likely. The whites of his eyes were caramel colored, but black in the center, distant and deep. He wore a perfectly round black hat with a band of silver and turquoise medallions, and several heavy bracelets in the same style on both arms. He played without looking at his cards, it seemed. He was looking at me the whole time, or through me, without appetite or desire or any form of interest I could understand. It made me wonder what he was thinking, not something I usually do.

Around midnight he had lost all he had, about eight hundred dollars, I think. He heaved himself up from his chair and left. In an hour or so he had returned, without his hat or the bracelets or the belt with the big silver-and-turquoise buckle. I don't think he'd had a watch to begin with. He started with a hundred fresh dollars in chips and by two in the morning he had won more than a thousand. He shoved eighty dollars' worth toward me for a tip, and carried the rest to the cage to cash out. Something changed in his look when he pushed out of his chair the second time, nothing measurable in his expression, but still some difference was being expressed. A bear might look at you that way if it wasn't hungry. A couple of hours later I saw him again across the floor. He was wearing the hat and all the rest he'd had when he first came in. He might have looked my way for a second, but his face was invisible under the hat's wide brim, the dark eyes blotted away in shadow.

I signed myself out and went to the restaurant: a sort of faux diner with Pullman décor, lots of chrome and red leatherette stools. In the town where I grew up there'd been a real one like that, made out of an actual railroad car, where my brother would buy me milk shakes sometimes. The casino's version had a slot machine wherever there was space for one, of course, and under the countertop in front of each stool was a video poker screen. I sat drinking straight whiskey out of a water glass, as I usually did at the end of my shift, watching the computer spool out endless hands of five-card draw beneath the smeary glass.

There are no televisions in a casino, lest any signal from the outside world should leak in—for the same reason that there are no clocks and no windows. But in the phony diner there were two, perched high in the corners at either end of the counter. The sound was almost always turned off, and I had scarcely looked at them before; perhaps I hadn't even known they were there. But that night, that morning, whenever it was, they were playing the fall of the towers, over and over, in rapturous silence. That image of Laurel swam across the screen again, flung to her knees, her back arched in a bow and her mouth a black hole, as if the Furies were lashing her breast with the scorpion whip. As if she were a Fury herself.

I was hungry then, so I ordered prime rib, so rare it was served in a pool of warm blood. Tammy frowned as she covered the poker screen with my plate, tucking a strand of her washed-out red hair behind an ear.

"I don't see how you can eat that," she said, or maybe, *I don't see how you can eat.*

7

I stopped at Wal-Mart on the way home, to buy some videocassettes. Another windowless, timeless box, a big casino. They have everything that money can buy. Something beautiful happened that I hadn't expected. To find the tapes I had to go where the televisions were. Hundreds of them, from tiny portables to panoramic home-theater screens, and all of them playing that same cascade of images. Before that spectacle all the mortals who had wandered into the building had been captured, as if turned to stone. They were prostrate, dumbstruck, leveled by awe. There must have been noise but I didn't hear it. I spun like a dancer among all those screens, letting the light play over my body. It made me feel pretty, which I seldom do.

I stayed in the trailer with the blinds drawn, crouched below my television cart, jabbing the pause button till the VCR spindles squealed. In four hours I had sculpted two perfect hours of tape, with no commentators or gabbling or crawls across the bottom of the screen. Then I sat back and watched. The planes bit chunks from the sides of the towers and the gorgeous sheets of orange flame roared up and the mortals flung away from the glittering windows like soap flakes swirling in a snow globe and the tower shuddered, buckled, blossomed and came showering down.

Raze it. Raze it. Again. Again.

I took off my clothing and stood naked before the full-length mirror screwed to the back of the bathroom door. My body has suffered few of the ravages the flesh of mortal women is heir to. There are few lines and little sagging. I've never had a problem with my weight. The breasts were always mere suggestion, barely rounding the line of the rib cage, still almost as high and firm as they were in my spring. My hair needs some chemical help to stay black. The hair around my vulva is gray, but that doesn't matter; when I fuck I do it in the dark.

The trailer rocked in the desert wind. I put on a shirt and some drawstring trousers. Outside it was once more night. I picked up the rifle and went into the desert.

8

Why I don't love the desert. Why I don't. Why I don't love. Where I grew up was wet and fecund and succulent green. Red clay country, slick with red mud and crawling with vine. Playing Indian, we'd streak our cheekbones umber with the clay. On the road, waiting for the lumbering yellow school bus, we would throw jagged little stones at snakes. Kudzu sprawled over everything, dragging down the trees.

No snow in winter, but rain, rain. Gullies washed red mud across the yard and the creek overflowed with snapping turtles and the fat, slick salamanders we used to call red dogs. Doors stuck shut and the windows warped and the panes beaded and streaked with rainwater till you felt like you were down in a diving bell. Summertime, the air was so thick that to breathe felt like drowning. We walked shellacked in thick layers of sweat. Every fold of skin stuck together, sucked apart.

Saturdays Dad or Terrell would push the mower snarling around the yard while indoors fans rattled and paddled the heavy air, and the black-and-white TV chattered in a corner of the living room. Momma cooked green beans all day till they were soft and gummy, with slick rings of white onion, red pepper, and spoons of bacon grease she squirreled up in a can. Out back was an A-frame garage with the white paint cracking and peeling off. Kudzu swarmed out from the woods behind, wrapped over the roof like a giant squid attacking a ship. One tentacle coiled around the attic window, its tip probing under the wooden frame.

Inside, an old tennis ball swung on a piece of fish-line so Dad could park the car just so, without smacking a bumper into the wooden steps at the back.

In the attic Terrell had his old Boy Scout sleeping bag spread on a yellowing strip of foam mat, smelling musty with the damp and the funk. In the corner a burned-up aluminum saucepan did what it could to catch the leak. The runner of vine that had forced the window spread suckers over the soggy wallboard. A few rusty nail points poked through the slanted boards of the roof. On other nails Terrell had hung the pellet gun and the old bayonet and the fake shrunken head he claimed was a real one. Hid in a cranny were half a pack of Newports, a deck of naked lady cards, a couple of miniature Jack.Daniel's somebody had got on an airplane once. He had a couple of box turtle shells and a small possum skull that still smelled of rot. Snake skins he'd found were tacked to the rafters, shivering slightly, if there was a draft. *Come up here, Mae,* my brother said. *I want to show you something.*

9

I got my rifle from a friend . . . more of an acquaintance, really. Fuck buddy, the kids call it nowadays. I could call him Pauley. We met when I was dealing at the Showboat, which was quite a long time ago.

Pauley lives in Vegas, as much as he lives anywhere. He spends a lot of time hopping back and forth to both coasts. He finds people; that's his gig. Apparently he's really good at finding people who don't want to be found, and often it's the last time that they ever do get found. Or the next to last time, in a lot of cases. Then some cases aren't so serious, I think, but I don't really know. I don't talk to Pauley much about his work.

The rifle was a used one, then. I knew that, and I knew that Pauley had taken a bit of a risk in letting me have it. It touched me that he trusted my discretion.

It was all over guns where I lived as a kid and by the time I was twelve I could knock a beer can off a fence post with Daddy's Smith & Wesson .38, do it any time I tried. Terrell and I would sneak out with the pistol, but I was a better shot than Terrell, come to think. That old .38 was just an average throw-down but Pauley's rifle, the one he gave me, was perfect all over, beautifully balanced and sighted to the last micron. We went out in the desert one night on the theory he was going to show me how to use this gun. I set an eight-ounce water bottle on his head and shot it off at thirty yards. It seemed risky to go for fifty yards by moonlight, even though the moon was full.

I'll hand it to Pauley, he didn't balk at this idea. I think we both had done some coke beforehand. Afterward, we went back to my trailer and fucked like panthers. In the dark, as I have said.

The water bottle lay on the pale sand with the water bleeding out through the hole I'd drilled through it. It was summer, and the sand was still hot even though it was nighttime, and in less than a minute the water stain around the bottle had leached away and the bottle itself was dry as a bone.

. . .

The clip of Laurel on her knees was 22.4 seconds long and after I had spent about a hundred hours watching it I thought once, thought twice, and called up Pauley. I told him as much as I could about Laurel without telling him the one thing that would have stopped even his heart. That was a tricky procedure, in fact. Pauley had his sentimental side, which maybe wasn't so surprising, and he seemed to think it was sweet that I wanted to look up a long-lost friend I'd seen on a 9/11 video. There was a certain amount of that kind of thing going on at the time, along with all the women suddenly falling in love with firemen.

It must have been a novelty for Pauley too, to be sent out to find somebody he wasn't expected to frighten or harm. And he was good, extremely good, at finding.

It turned out that Laurel was living under what used to be O——'s government name. I had to wonder what she was thinking, when she came up with that one.

10

Not so very long after it started, I began to realize that my brother was hardening me for something. I understood it better later, but even then I had the thought. And maybe even he knew too, or had some inkling. Whenever he'd sink me in another burning pool of pain, he was tempering me for what I'd later have to bear. Preparing me to meet my destiny.

Of course he was a mortal himself, and Thetis wasn't. But my brother died like a god! He took all his retainers with him—all. Except for me.

11

I still had all of O——'s old records, though probably most of them were scratched. His pictures on the jackets wrinkled with old spills. In the fold of a double album I found a couple of thirty-year-old pot seeds.

It had all come out on CD, of course, the instant they invented them. You could, I could, download them to your iPod or whatever.

I didn't try to listen to the records, in part because I didn't own a turntable anymore. I did slide one of the platters out, to look at the oily black surface. A puff of powdery cigarette ash came out of the sleeve ahead of the disc. A pale curved gash lay across the grooves of the first three tracks.

When I pushed the record back into the jacket, my eye lingered on something it had skimmed a thousand times before. Snaps from the recording session were printed on the cover, laid out in an artificially casual fashion, as if they'd fallen on the floor. There was O—— in the spring of his youth, an acoustic guitar balanced on one knee, looking with smiling, lively interest at something beyond the right edge of the frame.

The thing I hadn't previously attended to was a foot, down in the lower right-hand corner of the snapshot. A nicely shaped young foot with a high graceful arch, nail polish of such a dark crimson it was almost black, a gold-colored toe ring, and one of those higgledy-piggledy patterns Laurel used to draw on herself with henna back then.

Now there was a woman ahead of her time. I don't know how I'd never noticed that before.

As for the music of Orpheus, it was balm to everyone's wound. Your broken bones began to knit together when you heard it. Everyone turned toward it, like grass turns toward the sun.

12

La Brea Tar Pits. I couldn't have said exactly how I got there. If I had taken a bus down the coast or possibly come in a private vehicle, in exchange for private services along the way. I sat in half lotus on the concrete rim of the black sinkhole. It seemed jet black at first, deep as empty space, but the longer I looked at it the more I began to find a spectrum in the iridescence of the oily surface, like tendrils of dawn spinning free of the color of night. The tar pool absorbed my vision entirely and for a long time I had no thoughts at all. Nothing else was reaching my senses, although beyond the fence enclosing the pit were dump trucks and jackhammers and cranes, infernal engines clamoring to raise hell higher.

I felt D——'s eyes on me long before I looked up. By then I had a sense for it. I'd had a longish layover in Denver on my way here, and most recently I'd been up in the Tenderloin, *balling* for *bread*. Or being *balled*. For *bread*. Quaint terms they seem now, but then they were exotic, strange—back when Dad stalking the lawnmower around the soggy yard with a dead pipe clamped in his military jaws was supposed to be the very picture of normal.

I could feel D——'s look stroking over me with the tingling rasp of a cat's tongue. What there was to see. My unwashed hair long enough to pool on the concrete beside my thighs, the natural black of it dulled by dirt. I had on a tie-dyed T-shirt just sufficient to cover my ass when I stood up, and that was it; I had nothing under it, and only a scrap of macramé tied over the hips to reinforce the illusion that the T-shirt was a dress. My bare feet were calloused, grimy, cracked at the heel. I might have had a blown-out pair of high-top sneakers in my string bag, and what else? Half a banana, a jar of wheat germ, who knows. The bayonet I still had certainly, with the blade hidden in a fat roll of newspaper, the grip not looking much at all like an umbrella handle, I realized when D——'s eyes hesitated there.

There was a body on my back-trail, my very first bag of mortal bones. It worried me, because I hadn't yet figured out that nobody was going to miss that motherfucker, what a completely disposable person he was. D——'s look began to travel again, brushing my nipples under the cotton, grazing the edge of the T-shirt's hem, which stretched just enough to hide my bare snatch, then circling to number the knobs on my back. And there was something different about it. I didn't feel like I could just ball this cat and send him on his way, which had become sort of a universal solution in those days, whether I got paid for it or not. *A woman has two purses.* This look was like a doctor's touch, almost, with a tinge of the therapeutic in it—I had a sick tumbling thought of those do-gooders I'd sometimes met on my way, the ones who wanted to Clean You Up and Send You Home. But it wasn't quite that either. There was still a thread of desire in the look, and more than that, it was appraisal. By that I mean to say I felt valued, like D—— wanted to know me, to know what was in me, and what might come out.

I found myself looking for his reflection in the tar pit, but of course it didn't give any reflection—that was the whole point. I couldn't even see his shadow. Maybe he didn't cast one.

"That's where we all come from," D—— said. "Or is it where we're all going?"

The tar seemed to swirl in a pattern like paisley. Although D——'s efforts to sing were hopeless, his speaking voice was rich and resonant, and could make almost any bullshit seem wise until you thought about it.

I looked up at him then. D—— was a little small for his clothes, and another curious thing, he was covered up very completely considering that the weather was hot. The cuffs and collar of his Western-yoked shirt were tight with pearly snaps at the wrists and the throat, and his jeans were lashed into the fringed tops of high moccasin boots. He had dark wavy hair that just broke on his shoulders, that he had to keep tossing back all the time, like they all did, unless they went whole hog for the hippie headband. The famous Vandyke on the hungry jaw. His eyes, just a touch too close together, were electric, cobalt blue.

"You look troubled," he said, and held out his hand. Here's why I didn't laugh in his face. *Are you in trouble?* was a standard line to pick up a runaway, but there was something about this variation. Like instead of me being in it, the trouble was in me.

Why not. The hand was small, no bigger than mine, faintly calloused, slightly warm. But it was the eyes, I still admit it, that hit me where I lived. True, I was troubled and in trouble both. But, if D—— had an eye for weakness, he liked it mixed with strength.

At first I thought D——'s eyes were like my brother's. In time I realized that was wrong. All of it—the wine, the smoke, the trances—gave you back only what had been in you always. D——'s eyes were the reflection of my own.

13

"Shakespeare said that," I told Laurel, losing confidence before I got out all three of those words. I could see from the hesitation in her eyes that I was wrong, that I hadn't got the reference right, and hadn't really understood it either. I thought then that one was the purse you kept your cash in, while the second lay between your legs . . .

But Laurel had been to college, and not only that; she knew a number of things I didn't. All of a sudden she dropped to her knees and began to burrow in a milk crate that had been half covered by a swatch of the batik spread over her mattress. She came up with a book, already reading:

> Love is a bear-whelp born: if we o'erlick
> Our love, and force it new strange shapes to take,
> We err, and of a lump a monster make.
> Were not a calf a monster that were grown
> Faced like a man, though better than his own?
> Perfection is in unity: prefer
> One woman first, and then one thing in her.

Her laughter drew mine out of me, as if we were sharing some old secret. Bits of a title I could make out in splintered silver letters on the broken blue spine of the book she was holding, but those printed words meant nothing to me; it was all in the sound of her voice. Then she pulled me into it, catching her free hand around my waist. We propped on our elbows on the mussed covers of her low bed. Her finger traced the lines as she read them to me.

> Her swelling lips; to which when we are come,
> We anchor there, and think ourselves at home,
> For they seem all: there Sirens' songs, and there
> Wise Delphic oracles do fill the ear;
> There in a creek where chosen pearls do swell,
> The remora, her cleaving tongue doth dwell.

Gilt bells of laughter poured from her; it seemed the laughter as much as her lips that kissed me then, just grazing the corner of my mouth. Innocent as two little girls in Eden, she made it seem, so quick I'd have wondered if it had happened at all if not for the tingle that remained, sank deeper.

"But look—here's the part you mean." Laurel caught me by the nape of my neck to show me, saying the words with a husk catching in her throat.

Rich nature hath in women wisely made
Two purses, and their mouths aversely laid;
They then which to the lower tribute owe
That way which that exchequer looks must go . . .

I understood as much of this as I needed to. Enough to get us on our way. It wasn't the first time I'd been with a woman, but—

The salt taste of her was extraordinary; I haven't forgotten it even now. It was like I had some mineral deficiency and couldn't get enough. Behind my closed eyes was the picture of a red salt block for the cows across the road down home, and once I'd wormed under the fence, as a tiny girl, to get a lick of it for myself. My mother spanked me when I was caught, because it was *unsanitary* (smack!), *filthy* (smack!), *dirty* (smack!) and I almost wished she could see me now with Laurel, about to squirm right out of her skin from all the pleasure I was giving her, with that same red salt taste on my tongue, a scatter of cinnamon umber on her white froth, the ring of her laughter swelling into her transported cry.

14

So then one night Corey got caught chipmunking. Eye in the sky saw him packing his cheeks till it looked like the mumps. Corey had got a little too greedy. And the system wants all its pieces of silver. Counts them every day.

"Your country's in crisis," the pit boss told him. "We're all under attack here," Marvin said. "And now you *steal*."

All of us who could hear this line did our very best to look solemn and dour, though the truth was I wanted to break out laughing, or puke. It seemed to me all those little black globes in the ceiling were pressing down hard on the back of my neck. Like taking a few chips away from the company was some kind of betrayal of God and the flag and apple pie.

Not that I'd cry big tears for Corey. He'd ground up one Oxycontin too many, or he wouldn't have been so sloppy as to get picked off. I don't think anybody ratted him out. Eye in the sky just happened to see him—one little squirrel with too big of a nut. Corey was on the tall side, stooping and boney. He had sandy hair and thin skin that colored up fast. His ears were sort of pointy, and thin as parchment paper. He'd turned a deep purple by the time Marvin got through with him. Happily he didn't take all that long, but my nails had dug creases in the butts of my palms by the time he was done. Even though I had them cut back to the quick.

It was a bigger than usual night for some reason. Once Corey had cleaned out his crap and gone off, they brought Tammy to take over his table. She was glad to get out from the fake diner counter, glad of a chance at some extra money. But Tammy was never much of a dealer. I knew she wouldn't hold that table for long.

For some reason I thought about Corey again when I got into my car after work. He'd be soaking his sorrows in a bar on the road to Vegas, a windowless bunker known as the Deadwood. I went there once in a while with Pauley, and I think Corey lived nearby. He could take one of his thin pointy ears and crumple it up till the whole thing could be stuffed in the hole. I remember him trying to pick up girls with this trick, though I don't think he was ever very successful.

Or maybe he was balled up in a set of dirty sheets somewhere, trying to slow down his breath and his heartbeat, wondering where his next vial of pills would be coming from . . .

I don't know why I'd spend a second thought on Corey. Though the idea of him somehow abetting our

Enemies was idiotic enough to get under my skin. Hopefully Marvin wouldn't tack that course long. Marvin was normally a practical guy, decent enough to most in the pit. A company man, it goes without saying. I turned my car and aimed it toward the desert and my trailer.

15

I walked into the desert till the world began to curve, till the electric lights dropped behind the warp of the horizon. You can never get completely away from the light pollution of all those towns, but where I stopped the stars were brighter. Again, no moon.

No tire tracks here, but I found myself squatting next to somebody's lost muffler. It had been there so long there was nothing left but a lacey filigree of brownish rust. I could have blown the whole thing away like a globe of dandelion seeds. But I didn't touch it. Nearby, a flat spiny cactus reached across the pale sand. A handful of small bleached stones, worn smooth as coins, scattered without a pattern.

I hunkered motionless on my heels. I waited. Presently a cat appeared, stalking so slow I really couldn't perceive the movement. For a time I wasn't even sure that splotch back toward the glow of habitation wasn't just some inanimate object that had been there all night. But no. I couldn't see it move but I could see that it had moved. About the size of an ordinary housecat, though maybe, probably it had gone feral. A jackrabbit was frozen, crouched tight to the sand a few yards to my right, completely motionless except for the tips of its long ears revolving, searching for sound. The cat made no sound, but when it had come within a dozen feet, the rabbit got itself unstuck and bounded away at the same moment or a short hair before the cat launched itself hopelessly, too short, too late. The cat pursued anyway. Its silence was strict.

I couldn't even find any paw prints in the sand, that cat had moved so lightly. Just a couple of scuff marks where it landed from the mistimed pounce.

My back was sore, my thighs and calves cramped, from crouching motionless myself for so long. But still I tried to lay down my feet as soft and weightless as cotton balls, as I walked back toward the trailer park. Orion was there in the eastern sky, with his jeweled belt, and the sword jutting down from it. The dick, Laurel liked to call it, for a joke.

My hands were cold when I came inside, though it wasn't yet at all cold in the desert. My legs and my back were all right by then but my hands stayed stiff and I couldn't seem to warm or loosen them. If I got arthritis, I thought, I couldn't deal. I found a can of Tiger Balm and smeared a dab over my knuckles and palms, rubbing till the grease was all absorbed and the tingling menthol burn had faded. I knew I didn't really have arthritis.

I dialed the number Pauley had found for me. Two

rings, three rings, four. My thumb hovered over the reset button.

"Hello . . ."

The voice was recognizable, though not unchanged. That huskiness, and a drowsiness in it. Had I expected to wake her up? A shade of alarm, as from someone unexpectedly roused. The night sky was just beginning to shatter. I'd carried the cordless phone to a lawn chair on my wooden deck, where I sat looking over the predawn desert, beyond the diamonds of chain-link fence. It would be later on the East Coast, though. Full daylight there. Maybe it was a weekend, I don't know.

"Hello?"

Certainly, it was Laurel's voice. I began to imagine the lines between us, pictured the phone signal bouncing off some satellite up in the slowly lightening sky where my eyes were turned, my gaze dissipating like the beam of a flashlight you shine into the black night of the universe, disappearing there. I could feel her turning blindly toward the silence where my voice remained hidden. Like an antenna searching for a signal. A head tied up in a black silk bag.

When I came to, the sun was up and in the distance I could hear machinery grinding down a mountain. Building, razing, it never stopped. My clothes and my skin were coated with a fine stone grit. The dial tone droned from the wireless handset I held cupped in both hands, clasped into my navel. Laurel hadn't said another word.

16

She told me she'd once seen D—— bring a dead bird back to life. In my mind, I didn't believe it. Laurel had been tripping, maybe, or simply misunderstood what she saw.

Back home a redbird flew into our picture window and knocked itself out. The four of us sitting just inside, eating Sunday pancakes. The Mom-thing had her fork arrested halfway to her mouth. Across the table I could see her gullet trembling.

So Terrell went out and picked up the bird from the damp cold ground. It was early spring, it seems to me; the trees were in bud and the air getting fresher. At first light there'd be a lingering chill but after sunrise the warmth strengthened. I'd seen Terrell with dead animals before but this redbird wasn't dead. And he did have that gentleness in him somewhere, sometimes—it was not often it surprised me. He cradled the bird in his hands and teased its crest back into place with a fingertip. We watched him. Them. After a minute or so the bird came completely unstunned and flew off.

* * *

I too with my own eyes have seen it, when D—— struck the desert floor with his staff and brought everything all at once into bloom. In one stroke the desert was writhing with green and when we crushed the grapes into our mouths they had already turned to wine.

I am your love, D—— used to say. He had that gentleness in him too. Surprising. Though when he shared the love with you, he made it hurt enough that you knew he was there.

So I didn't really believe Laurel's story, but somehow I did see it through her eyes. I can't say what I mean to say. It was more like she kissed the dry surface of my brain and made it fertile. In the green crystal of her vision I saw D—— stoop to lift the dead bird from the sand. Brown and inert as if it had never lived at all, hard as a clod or any old piece of shale from the desert. D——'s hair blew clean and silky into his eyes and he shook it back unconsciously and lowered his head again over his cupped hands to breathe on the bird, warming it with his breath till it took on all the colors of the spectrum. It lived, and perched on D——'s raised finger. He raised his arms like an apostle. In that instant I could see the hot red heart of the bird, fluttering inside like moth wings. Then it took the air and flew, away into the arid slopes of the Santa Susana Mountains to the north.

Then I knew the same fire burned in Laurel's head as burned in mine.

17

From the campsite, Terrell took me out to hunt stuff. We'd gone floating on the river; two canoes and two tents. The Mom-thing didn't like it much, but she'd go along with Dad for a day or so. Terrell liked it. I don't remember exactly how I felt. Terrell had been a Boy Scout and dropped out after six months because he thought it was dumb, he said, and also I think he had managed to get into some kind of trouble at the church where they had their dumb meetings in the basement. But he was still wearing some rags and tags of Scout uniform on that river trip. It made him look sort of like a soldier drummed out of his regiment (there was something like that on TV at the time), and I think we both found this appearance somehow bold and a little romantic.

Terrell was good at finding things. He had sharp eyes and spent a lot of time in the woods. He found skulls and snake skins and live snakes in season and all that he found he would carry home. He found dead animals surprisingly often. They might not all have been dead when he first found them.

But I don't see how he could have killed the longhorn cow . . . way back in the woods on the ridge behind our house and lot, sloughed down in a red clay gulley, with tendrils of kudzu already wrapping over the rotting piebald flanks. It was the horns that attracted him, me too I'll admit. He made me help wrestle the half-rotting head back down the hill and through the brush into our yard. Both of us too proud to puke, just barely.

The Mom-thing went completely crazy: a screaming, slobbering, falling-down fit. Terrell took the rap for it, claimed the whole thing was his doing, while I crept under the porch and hid behind the crisscross lattices. She made him swear he'd dump it back wherever it was *in hell you found it*. In fact he only carried it across the creek out back and stuck it on an abandoned pump-house where nothing could get it for a month or so, till finally it was rotted dry and bleached clean enough for him to sneak it up the back stairs of the garage.

You could pull the horns off then. They came away easily from the porous bone. Each was a foot and a half long, and curling. Inside there lingered, for years and years, the faintest smell of rot.

I wasn't much good at finding stuff, but I liked going out with Terrell. I did find minié balls sometimes—there were such a lot of those from the old battles of the War Between the States, sunk in the furrows like dead seeds. A time or two Terrell dropped an arrowhead ahead of where I was going to walk, plain out in the open where I'd be sure to find it. I knew that he had done that, but I didn't say.

Water maples screened the campsite on the riverbank. Through the trees we could smell the freeze-dried stroganoff that Dad was heating on the Coleman stove, while the Mom-thing, doubtless, worried about water moccasins and wished that she could take a bath and curl her hair. It would have been early fall, I think, with the leaves just changing on the trees. Fat purple berries buttoned pokeweed, and the fencerows were thick with sumac turning the colors of rust.

We were walking a field that had lain fallow for at least a year. I wouldn't have noticed that at the time, but Terrell would. I remember now the hummocks of old rows we stepped across, decaying corn-stubble overgrown with weeds. Terrell started along the fence posts, eyes tracking the ground at the edge of old turned earth. I went the other way, across the open space.

In opposite directions, we quartered the field, then finally turned back to meet each other in the middle. It must have been fairly dim by then—the fireflies were starting to come out—so it's sort of surprising either one of us saw it, much less both at the same time. The stone tip breaking the dirt beneath a corn tussock like a fin. Maybe a flaked edge of it caught the remains of the light.

This is ours, Terrell said.

Not mine, *mine!* None of that old tug of war. Both our hands covered the stone blade, but with a kind of reverence. We knew already it was different, special. The stone was different from all our other points, black, smooth, and darkly shining. It had been made in a distant place, before it was carried here. Out of darkness and old night. A firefly winked phosphorescent green as it walked among the fine pale hairs of Terrell's forearm. I could feel the warmth of his hand spreading toward mine, across the obsidian blade. We did not yet have all our secrets on that evening, though they were coming near.

When we had been much smaller, really small, Terrell, playing Indian, used to take me out in the woods and tie me to a tree. He'd go off for a while, not long I think, then return in the role of some frontiersman for my rescue.

I don't remember anything, really, about the time in between.

The Mom-thing whined and fretted when she learned about it. It's not *natural.* It's not *right.* Daddy brushed off her objections. Kid stuff. They'll grow out of it. It was normal, Daddy told her, and maybe, up to a point, that was so.

Up to a—

Terrell didn't have much of a narrative for this game,

or if he did I have forgotten what it was. The binding and loosing was exquisite. A throb that moved deep from the core of me and spread to my outermost edge. I didn't know the name for it but I knew you kept it in the dark.

18

In the morning we could hear D—— chunk-chunking an acoustic guitar in the lodge, stopping and starting again, repeating a phrase and trying different words against it. A couple of girls sat cross-legged on the dirt, smudged faces turned up and their mouths open, listening to the sounds that trickled out through the gap in the window. Laurel caught my hand and pulled me away, across the half-closed circle of tent and shack and gutted school bus. Ned was working on a dune buggy engine, with a stringy guy wearing colors of the Pagans motorcycle gang. The biker straightened up to watch us away. I didn't look back but I could feel his eyes like pinholes on either side of my spine.

We passed the barn and the corral. One cowboy was brushing down a horse and another trundling a barrow of manure. The place still functioned as a dude ranch, sort of; a few people came to rent horses and ride the dry hills.

Laurel wrinkled her nose at the bright greenish smell of the manure. "Come on," she said. "We'll go down to Clive's house. There'll be food."

The old man Clive, who owned the ranch, sat on a cement stoop outside his cabin, full in the sun, wearing a big Stetson hat and square dark glasses. A blind man's cane lay between his legs, wrapped with red electrical tape. Creamy squatted on the cement to the left of his seat, with Clive stroking her hair as if she were a cat. She seemed to like it. His hands were wrinkly, liver-spotted, very large. He had a pleasant sort of smile, beneath the black lenses and blind eyes.

Crunchy was frying eggs with corned beef hash in a black iron skillet in Clive's kitchen. "Share the love!" Laurel told her, with her delirious smile. "The People *share.*" Crunchy shook back her hair and shrugged, gave me a blank look when Laurel told her my name. That look was common enough among D——'s People.

Crunchy divided the food on paper plates. We ate around the stoop with Clive, not bothering to bring out chairs from inside. Crunchy and Creamy put an amazing amount of ketchup on their food, stirring it into a crimson porridge. They both had sandy, sort of wavy hair, and they dressed like twins, with yarn vests over their blue work-shirts, though they weren't actually related. Sometimes they were both there together; sometimes they worked it as a relay. D—— had told them they should keep Clive happy, which he seemed to be.

"Creamy balls him," Laurel told me, once we'd walked out of earshot of the place. "She says he's good."

If she wanted that to weird me out it didn't. I'd been

there, done it, whatever it took. What was weird was this old-time Western street we all of a sudden seemed to be on. All weather-beaten clapboard buildings, wooden porches with spooled posts. A pharmacy, a saddle shop, a jail, and a saloon . . .

"What is this?" I said. "It's like we're in some movie."

"Well, *yeah* . . ." Laurel flashed her smile at me, pushed open the swinging saloon doors. Through them was nothing, just more chaparral. The street was a set, the flats propped up with two-by-sixes wedged from the backs of them into the ground.

I started laughing. Laurel was too. Then we were chasing each other in and out of the dummy doors, up and down the pretend street, crouching to take aim and fire at each other with forefinger and cocked thumb. Laurel actually said *bang bang* when she did this action. Finally we slumped together, breathless and gasping, against the back of the saloon flat.

"Watch out," I said. "We'll knock it over."

Laurel couldn't seem to stop laughing. Then a motor coughed to life and she did stop, turning her head to the sound, alert, for a second, as a fox. They'd got the dune buggy going, I assumed.

We went swinging out through the saloon doors together, bumping our hips. Then froze, for there was someone at the far end of the street, the morning sun behind her, long legs set like a gunslinger's. Really a beautiful woman, like a star. She had on jeans and an orange tank top and there was a sort of snake bracelet clasped to her upper arm. Her long hair was crisp and spiky like straw and in the sun it was the color of gold. She had high cheekbones and the eyes of a cat, and though she was certainly looking our way, she didn't seem to see us.

"Who's that?" I said, and caught myself whispering.

"That's Eerie." Laurel linked her arm through mine to turn us away. "She's on her own trip. Don't think about her."

19

When we met at the tar pits wasn't the first time D——
and I had occupied the same space. Maybe the first time
we saw each other truly. But our paths had crossed
before, and not only in the Haight . . . where D—— had
been quite a visible figure, with his garlands and his
maidens. But he knew the Tenderloin as well as the
Haight, and so did I.

I'd walked by the house on Cole Street a time or two.
Seen an auburn-haired girl in a macramé vest leaning out
the bay window on the second floor, dangling a chain of
clover blossoms that nearly grazed the top step below. I
might even have been inside the place for a party, once
or twice, but my memory of that time's a little unclear,
though certainly the parties were better with the Airplane and the Dead. I don't think I went to D——'s
classes on Cole Street, though it seems that I knew they
were happening, through word of mouth, or maybe
there were posters. The same kind of rap we would hear
on the ranch. At the peak of the Haight scene, D——
couldn't really compete with the rock stars, not when

they were all just over the next block. To get the People to pay proper attention, he had to lead them into the desert.

Not that I was paying much attention at the time, but I could see the nucleus of the People forming then. The group around D—— had its own queer vibe already, the hum of everyone thinking the same tight gnarly set of thoughts. I'd feel it when I passed their house, or when they sometimes used to take over the Calm Center of the Psychedelic Shop, and even at free concerts in the Panhandle, though in those circumstances their clustered knot of energy tended to get broken up and rearranged by the movements of much bigger crowds and everything the music let loose.

I wasn't hearing the voices then, or they weren't saying much to me. Only my name sometimes. *Mae. Mae . . .* I hadn't yet been seized by the notion that the voices Laurel and I both heard were coming from D——, or through him. They gave me no more than half-formed syllables, sighing on the wind . . .

I didn't really live anywhere then. None of us did, or hardly anyone. We washed in and out of the crash pads like surf, or slept in the parks on the warm summer nights. A night in jail was always a possibility, but they didn't have cells enough to keep anybody too long. And there was a crib down in the Tenderloin that Louie let me use, if I was working.

There's a picture in my mind of D—— in the Panhandle, a bandanna knotted around his neck, his hair and his expression soft, his eyes half shut, blissed out on the music. A girl or two draped over him, surely—Creamy and Crunchy were already there, or maybe one of them was Stitch. It must have been O——'s big free show in the park, when O—— was in the prime of his glory, those brilliant days before Eerie was lost, and the sunset gilded his half-breed skin, and he raised the guitar and tilted it to the sun so the strings flowed away in red rivers of light . . .

Seeing D—— in a different context was like seeing a different guy—he had that chameleon quality to him, though I did know he was the same. I was leaving the Ellis Street crib at first light and saw him there with Louie on the corner of Hyde. Louie had probably been up all night, was still tricked out in his velvet bell-bottoms and the tall felt hat with the crazy feather. But D—— was the scarier of the two of them that day. His eyes were small and really hard and I could see, in the harsh early light, the lines that prison had drawn on him. There was a knot between his brows where later he would cut the cross.

There's two cats that know each other's business, I was thinking, and I didn't look at them for more than a flash. I was already walking the other way, so D—— couldn't have seen much more than my back.

But they did know each other's business. And D——
would have known, that day at the tar pits, what had happened to Louie not so long before. So he knew me
already, or one face of me. In a way, he already knew
who I was.

20

"Give me a penny," Laurel said.

"I don't have any thoughts," I told her, and she smiled. The radiant explosion of it—it seemed to me back then her smile was like the sun.

"It's unlucky if you don't," she said, and took her hand from behind her back. On her plump palm lay a big lock-blade Buck knife, a beautiful one with brass bolsters and brass-headed screws in the brown hardwood handle. Expensive too—I knew the price, because Terrell had always wanted one and never had the money to buy it.

"I already have a knife," I said. It occurred to me I had been seeing a few of these Buck knives around the ranch of late. For example, Creamy and Crunchy each wore one, in a black web sheath strapped to her skinny hip. Stolen, I guess, for money was tight. Somebody must have boosted a box of them.

"Oh yeah?" Laurel said, her eyes flashing a challenge.
"Yeah . . ."

I didn't hesitate for more than two seconds before I dipped into the bundle I brought when I came. The bayonet was clean, though I hadn't had the blade exposed since I left San Francisco. I held it bolt upright in my hand, my thumb set in the steel ring where the tip of the rifle was supposed to go.

"*Oh,* yeah . . ." Laurel's eyes had widened, though not for long; I saw her touch her upper lip with the pink point of her tongue. Then she stooped to her side of the bed and pushed a knot of colored scarves off a long flat sandalwood box. Inside was a knife as long as mine, with a rippling blade like water.

A kris, I'd later learn was the name of it. Laurel had pictures of Malays sticking themselves with these things when they danced, possessed by their demons. At the moment I didn't give a goddamn whatever the thing was called.

Laurel's eyes glimmered as she stepped around the foot of the bed, striking toward me in slow motion, and I parried, slowly, very careful—I didn't much care about not getting cut but I did care about not cutting Laurel. The bayonet was sharp enough to shave, I knew, after the hundred hours Terrell had put into the edge.

We were moving around each other, eyes on fire, our lips just parted. Strike, parry, parry, strike. The electric *ting* of metal meeting metal. My bones were throbbing with excitement—current spouting up to the top of my head through the soles of my feet. D—— had been teaching new uses of fear. She came down overhand with the flat of the wavy blade and I didn't block it this time, let it reach me, just denting into the top of my left breast. The bayonet swung around lazily to the right and came softly to rest on the skin of her throat. I hadn't controlled it quite enough or maybe I'd controlled it just perfectly, for there among her cinnamon freckles rose a bright red bead of blood.

Laurel shivered, as if she'd seen the blood bead reflected in my eyes. She touched the spot and raised her finger toward me and I tasted her blood from the whorls of the tip. When we kissed it was like springwater pouring from her mouth to mine. I don't know where the knives got slung—lucky neither of us was impaled when we fell, when we threw each other onto the bed. Laurel came out of her clothes like a piece of ripe fruit and we were slithering all over each other like a pair of wet squid and I plunged to raise her pearl on the tip of my tongue—

Afterward, I seemed to hear a voice explaining to me why the knives had helped, how they solved the frustration I often felt at the sheer painlessness of doing it with Laurel . . .

She stretched a languid arm to the floor and came up with the folded Buck again.

"Take it," she said. "D—— wants you to have it."

So I did.

21

Terrell pressed the bayonet against my cheek. Sometimes I think I feel it still: the cool triangular impression of the tip into my flesh. A tenderness there, in my still impressionable body, in my brother's attitude or even somehow in the metal blade itself.

Don't tell, he said. His heart beat quick against my ribs. His softest voice, strangely fond, which let us know the value of our secret. *I'll kill you if you tell.*

22

It wasn't that D—— wore the mask. D—— *was* the mask. The living face of god among us, empty eyeholes boring backward into the dark infinity of the universe beyond.

It wasn't always just his con and shallow cruelty. When love stood up among the People, he was father, mother to us all. At times there was great gentleness in him, and great joy. I saw him clothed in his divine glory, saying, *I bring not peace, but a sword.*

* * *

After dark we all piled into the old Ford Fairlane one of the cowboys let us use. I was wearing a white shirt, and Crunchy sent me back to get a dark one.

Stitch was driving, with Crunchy shotgun. Creamy in back with Laurel and me. We went south to the Ventura Highway, then cut over to the coast and rolled down Highway 1, toward Santa Monica. Stitch was a good driver, fast and tight to the curves. We all got high on a couple of joints Crunchy rolled us out of a plastic sandwich bag.

"Zig-Zag Wanderer," Creamy said as she crumbled

the last shreds of roach out the window, and everybody laughed for no good reason, except for Laurel, who curled sideways and put her head in my lap. It was too dark to see the water from the cliffs, although the stars seemed very bright out there, more like flares than pinpoints, though that would have been the grass.

Stitch stopped, finally, in a parking lot overlooking Muscle Beach, but we didn't get out of the car. A song of O——'s was on the tinny AM radio, one of the slow dark ones. It seemed to stretch out tacky and brown as caramel.

"What are we doing exactly?" I finally said. I had such a case of cotton mouth it was hard to get the words out. D—— had given us a mission of some kind—*Go slither,* he'd said, but I didn't know that part of the code and now when stoned I remembered the words they echoed and shivered inside the dark and cavernous mouth-hole of the mask. Stoned, I couldn't recall if D—— had audibly pronounced those words or if they'd simply surfaced in our minds.

Laurel butted her head into my ribs, like a lamb; she didn't say anything.

"Waiting for bedtime," Crunchy said, and she and Stitch both laughed.

Stitch drove us up into the Santa Monica Mountains then. The Fairlane had a spotlight built into the vent window on the driver's side, and Stitch flashed a couple of oncoming cars with it, until Crunchy told her to stop. "You'll get the pigs after us," Crunchy said.

Crunchy rolled another one, and maybe it was out of a different bag, because all of a sudden I was a lot more stoned than before, like it was real trip weed. We went up and down the canyons. It was late now and there weren't any other cars. Stitch pulled off, tucking the Fairlane behind a mailbox, and cut the engine and lights. The car ticked cool. It filled up with a single thought shared by the five of us, and though I couldn't have said it I felt like I knew what it was.

Crunchy got out and walked up the driveway. In her dark clothes we couldn't see her once she'd gone a few yards past the hood. The canyons were shady and the starlight didn't come through. She disappeared into this jet-black darkness as though injected into an artery. But after a few minutes a dog started barking, and Crunchy came back, just a little faster than she'd gone.

Stitch slipped the car into neutral and let it roll back onto the road before she started the motor. She drove about a quarter mile before she put the lights back on. I didn't have any idea where we were anymore, but Stitch seemed to know her way around. There was a sort of static charge inside the car; it tingled like the moment before sex. I had an idea what we were looking for now, like maybe a house without a dog.

We stopped again and Crunchy got out, and this time

she didn't come back for a bit. No one said anything, but after a while Stitch reached softly for the door handle and at that moment I felt some kind of pulse inside my head, like a thought from Crunchy had landed there, except I had the strange idea that maybe the thought had really come from D——, way back at the ranch. Like the phantom voice I sometimes barely used to hear was now ventriloquized by him.

Laurel sat up silently, alert and keen. We were all barefoot. The asphalt of the driveway was still just faintly warm from the day.

Fear, excitement, fear, just different words for the same thing. D—— had been rapping a lot lately about what fear could do for you. It was like we were all flying on big hits of fear as we filed in silence around the curve of the drive to the point where Crunchy waited, half hidden by a trellis, watching the stucco wall of the house all spangled ivory color in the starlight.

A cat came out from under the sash of a cracked window. It dropped on all fours to the patio tiles and looked at us indifferently, then padded off around the corner of the house.

Crunchy darted to the house wall, and crouched below the window. My mind caught on the quick electric stops and starts of her movement, light and crisp as a skink. She slithered up the wall and poured herself through the crack in the window the cat had come out of. There wasn't any word for it but *slither*.

In the next instant Creamy had done the same and I felt a pull to go after them, like they were two magnets pulling me along. I could definitely fit into the crack they'd taken, though Laurel, plumper and wider in the hips, might have had more trouble. A thought stopped me. Stitch's empty hand was on my arm.

A glass door slid open, farther down the wall, though I couldn't see anyone behind it, just a slash of darkness, colorless. Beside the opening the heavy blackness of the glass seemed to spin whorls of oil-spill radiance in it, though maybe that was because I was stoned. We went crouching toward the gap, we slithered through. The interior was all Danish modern, glass and flat planes and staggered levels. We slithered about, keeping to the shadows and low to the floor. Crunchy and Creamy were the best at it. You couldn't seem to see them at all till one of their heads came up and froze, like the probing head of a snake.

Fear is a man's best friend. I could taste it like blood in the back of my throat. My heart was beating like a kettle drum, like the heart of all the People beat in us and in me. Why couldn't they hear that? I was wondering, except I didn't know who *they* might be, until we'd all slithered into the bedroom one by one, following Crunchy and Creamy. Two Beautiful People were sleeping there, in the starlight pouring through another half-open glass door. A sheer white curtain quivered in the breeze. They slept naked in a tangle of expensive-looking sheets. The man's mouth open, not quite snoring. The woman's breasts looked marble in the light. She reminded me of Eerie, though she didn't look like Eerie; it was just the same incredibly high standard of being beautiful.

With the tiniest snick, Crunchy's Buck knife opened, pricked upright in her boney hand. *Fear*. She'd wake them. Surely they would wake. The shadow of the knife lay on the woman's navel. Crunchy's dry tongue flicked in and out like a snake's.

"Duh," the woman said, and stirred a little, her closed eyelids fluttering. "Duh . . . *Doormat*." She turned and nuzzled against her lover, gouging deeper into sleep.

Laurel had taken a handful of spoons from the kitchen and now she switched them with some jewelry that was laid out on the vanity. We didn't actually steal anything, though. Laurel put the jewelry where she'd found the spoons, and Creamy filled a cereal box with dry cat food and Stitch put a picture from the wall on the coffee table and propped a book from the table on the nail where the picture had been.

We slithered out. Halfway across the patio the word *doormat* pulsed into my mind and I went back and turned the doormat around so the WELCOME would be upside down.

Stitch let the car roll down the canyon. For a minute it felt like we were falling out of a plane. Then Stitch started the car by popping the clutch even though she had the key in the ignition all along, and all of us started laughing all at once.

"Doormat," Creamy said, through the giddy laughter. "Doormat—that was a good one, Mae."

I could begin to feel my head coming back to me then, away from the People, and it was odd how I didn't really want it to.

"Tell me what that was all about?" I said.

"Higgledy-piggledy," Laurel said, still laughing, wrinkling her nose as I hugged her, both of us feeling the flush of fear as it changed the name we put on it.

"Just a little." Laurel giggled. "A little higgledy-piggledy for the pretty piggy people in the morning."

23

So it was told by Epitherses, returning from his voyage, the ship on which he was embarked lay opposite the isle of Paxi, becalmed, when out of the dark forest lining the shore a voice called for the Egyptian pilot Thamus, at which the passengers stopped drinking their wine. Thamus heard the call three times before he answered; the voice then boomed out to him: *When you come opposite to Palodes, announce that Great Pan is dead.* Then Thamus was not sure at all if he would do as he was enjoined, but after some reflection thought that he would let chance or destiny decide the question—if the wind was fresh when they came near Palodes, he would sail past while holding his tongue, but in the event they were again becalmed there, the longboat drifting, turning in slack tide; Thamus then with some reluctance raised his voice loud across the dark plane of the water, and when they heard him there was tumult among those gathered on shore, with cries of wonderment and sorrow.

Great Pan is dead.

So too, many oracles have failed, and what had branded immortality in me—

The god that had once lived in D—— had left him long ago. The shell of him still lay in bondage, under D——'s government name. The name of a petty criminal, thief and pimp, a murderer only by proxy. From his own being he had nothing to offer except the cheapest mortal madness.

✦ ✦ ✦

The first casino where I worked was a round room. Once the door had closed behind you, it was near impossible to get out if you didn't know your way. A tight interminable circle, all mirrors and buzzers and flashing lights. The promise of money and nothing but money, the vacant tokens of exchange. So you let yourself be lured along, forgetting everything outside the lure.

The worst was it was always Christmas there. They made everyone wear Santa hats, and for the girls, red miniskirts with a trim of fake white fur.

There were rats there too, in the round room, the kind with four paws and snaky tails. I seem to remember one that ran and ran, with the dogged determination of a pit boss making his rounds, only with no purpose, around and around the edge where the circled wall met the carpeted floor. A flashback, maybe. I don't know. In those days I was coming off a lot of long strange trips. But it is a realistic rat in my memory. It wasn't washed over in op-art graphics and it didn't wear a Santa hat or cap and bells; it offered no anthropomorphic detail whatsoever.

An ordinary brown rat, the bearer of plague, in a trap large enough to allow it to run. Its eyes black pinholes into nothing; they stared relentlessly forward along the continuous curve.

· · ·

There's only one way out of this.

· · ·

What I mean to say is that no story matters. Not even the tales we have told of the gods. In two billion years the sun will have burnt this world into cinders. What I mean to say is there's nothing but this. This. Nothing. This.

24

The black knife was our secret and our treasure. We never showed the blade to either of our parents. The Mom-thing would have taken it away for fear we'd harm ourselves, we thought, and Dad would have wanted to sell it as a rarity.

It had come a long way and both of us knew it. Terrell, ordinarily no scholar, went to the library and boned up. The stone might have come from volcanoes out west, the Sierra Nevada or Medicine Lake. Points and blades like the one we had found were traded by Indians all over the continent. But Terrell liked to think ours came from South America. Had maybe been used, on top of some Aztec ziggurat, to carve out a living, beating human heart.

Terrell carved a handle from a stub of deer antler he'd squirreled up in the loft above the garage since he'd found it in the woods a year or so before. At the library he looked up diagrams that showed how the Indians had set about it. He was a long time filing a tight notch in the yellowed bone, and binding blade to shaft with strings of fresh, wet hog gut. I watched him, studied him while he worked. A rare thing to see him so absorbed. He had the same precisely focused attention as when he pulled the wings off flies. That rapt and ravenous concentration he always gave to hurting me. I bit my lips and held the stone blade while he did it. Sometimes there'd be a hairline cut across my palm when we were done. It helped me take the pain, and to withstand the pleasure that was braided with the pain.

Blade and bone were perfectly balanced. The warty curve of antler seemed to fit my hand exactly, the butt of my palm resting snug against the spreading base where it had once sprung from the skull of the buck. Terrell, possessive of most of his things, shared this weapon equally with me. The blade was a glossy smooth black, like glass, and if we turned it at a certain angle to the light, we saw flecks of gold drifting deep down inside it, like warm stars in a faraway galaxy.

Walking in the woods one day I came across the flayed cat in the fork of a tree. Eviscerated, a flat cat, reduced to the merest profile of itself. Its hide so dry it had grown harder than the bone. The shrunken skin pulled back the jaws and bared the needle teeth in what appeared to be a silent scream.

25

O—— pursued Eerie across the Styx and raised her up from her bier of death and led her back, for a little while, to the light and the warmth of the sun. But Eerie had eaten the food of death, and so she was bound to return to the shadows and the cold, there to remain forever . . .

Ευρυδηθε! O—— wailed then. *Ευρυδηθε* . . . That was her secret name. The same four syllables I still hear sometimes, crying in the desert.

After O—— had lost Eerie once and for all, he sang to us that we should kill our parents. But we had already done that, my brother and I—we killed them with our actions.

26

"I think you're hung up on your brother," D—— told me as soon as Laurel had left the room. It surprised me that he'd say that—it really kind of set me back. His usual line with the girls was that they had a father hang-up. An easy con—you didn't have to be Sigmund Freud to suppose that most of the ragged company of runaways D—— was gathering to himself had had some problem with their fathers, somewhere along the way.

I'd been with the People for two or three weeks— among them though not entirely one of them. Laurel delivered me to D——'s room in the lodge herself. I suppose I must have been expecting it. Yes, I certainly had been expecting it from the start, but D—— had hardly seemed to look my way since he first picked me up at the tar pits and brought me here, so I was left to wonder if he wasn't really interested, if after all he didn't really care . . .

Every pimp has that same bag of tricks. And I knew it well, but it didn't help me.

Laurel turned her eyes demurely down and strolled

out of the room, with a sweet little swing to her hips. I was aware that D—— wasn't watching her go.

The lodge had been used for a dining room, I think, back when the ranch served overnight guests. It was an octagon-shaped building, with a central fireplace and a round stone chimney that shot up through the cupola on top, which D—— had taken for his room. The cupola had an uninterrupted line of windows wrapping around all its eight sides, so there was a lot of light. D—— was reclining on his bed, draped in a striped blanket like an Indian brave, or a Roman in a toga, or the sheik of freaking Araby, for all I know.

What he had said disarmed me somehow. I'd made a success of not thinking about Terrell since I left.

D—— sat up and shook back his hair. It was silky today, and he looked gentle, all over somehow. The shoulder the blanket didn't cover looked smooth as milk to me.

When he stood up, I looked down at his bare feet on the wooden floor. I didn't like that I was doing that; I remembered how Laurel had turned her eyes down before leaving, and I thought I should have found D——'s eyes and held them, made him be the one to look away.

I felt Laurel pulse in the back of my mind. Only the tone of her voice, no word. Below the frayed hem of the blanket, D——'s calves were covered with a surprising amount of long fine hair, like angora.

"I know," he said. He came to me and touched me then, not much, maybe lifting my chin with a fingertip. His eyes were the deep fluid blue of the Gulf Stream and they seemed to see all the way into me, to read all the history carved on my core, so that I felt that he really did know.

"I can break that down for you," D—— said. "If you let me."

He touched me a little more, backing me against the chimney. I could feel the rough stone on my bare back and the backs of my legs, my whole nakedness spreading against the stone, and I still don't know how that came about, because I surely must have been wearing something when I went there.

"I'll be your brother to you," D—— said. "Will you let me?"

Then the ivy came boiling out of the cracks in the masonry and wrapped around my limbs and bound them—the ivy crawled over me like snake skin—and D—— was in me everywhere, not just the purses but my brain and my bloodstream too, and we were inside each other so completely it seemed that we could never come apart, and I was crying out my consent so loud they could have heard it on the highway.

. . .

It was hard to return to Laurel after that, because that was no ordinary con. D—— really had broken something down in me, and known me in ways that no stranger could know, and occupied a place in me that only my brother had touched before. A place that Laurel couldn't really reach.

And of course I knew that Laurel had her thing with D—— as well. From now on that would have to lie between us.

27

My brother put his palms on the slight swellings where my breasts would be, and told me in a husky croon how Indians would have cut two straps of flesh, there where his hands lay moist and warm above the shriveled beans of my nipples—they'd thread those slits with leather thongs lashed to a pole, then make me dance until I tore my own flesh free. In those days Terrell didn't really know which Indians were which and had the most mixed-up ideas of what they did. The Sun Dance was all jumbled up with Shawnee or Iroquois torture, then reassigned to Cherokees who'd once lived more or less where we did then. Not that Indians ever tortured women anyway, and not that the confusion made any difference to what we were about. These fantasies didn't need to make more sense than dreams did, and we didn't dare to take them out of fantasy. Terrell only hurt me inside, where it didn't show.

Already he had his peculiar fascination for those Indian captives who were proud to take the punishment without flinching. A brave who'd seat himself on the spit, unforced, unbound, tranquilly smoking a pipe while his own flesh roasted. With that image raised before me, I learned to go toward pain like a warrior.

We used to smoke together afterward, Terrell and I, the Newports we had filched from Mom. Those were the only times I ever smoked tobacco; in other situations I never felt the urge. Two or three times a week we'd have a couple of hours alone after school, before Dad came home from work, the Mom-thing off at some meeting or club. We'd lie covered with the musky sleeping bag, paired filaments of smoke rising up from our nostrils, wreathing themselves among the snake skins that shivered from the rafters, first blue, then gray, then finally vanishing into the heavy air. My head gradually coming back together from where it had been scattered by our deeds, because whenever he did what he wanted a part of me would leave my body to hover in the sky, far above the peeling tarpaper shingles but still able to observe the girl getting fucked by her brother, to see and hear how she moved and moaned, writhing under the onslaught of sensations she didn't even know how to distinguish as pleasure or pain.

And afterward, my head would be blank, empty as two halves of a vase, glued back together. Sometimes a voice appeared in the vacancy.

. . . Mae . . . Mae . . .

. . . Ευρυδηθε . . .

I made nothing of that then. By nightfall, by supper-time, I wouldn't remember that echo in the hollow of my skull.

Sometimes I heard a voice saying . . . I couldn't make it out. Or maybe it only made sound, without ever naming.

And I seemed to feel the bayonet stabbing and stabbing, impaling something that first resisted and then gave way to a lurching emptiness inside, so that I bashed the heel of my fist against the spot where the hilt stopped. The shock of it up my arm to the shoulder, over and over again.

Terrell whetted the bayonet relentlessly, till it was sharp enough to shave. He let me try it on his calf, the silver edge of it bringing away the stiff dark curls from the pale skin, like at a hog-killing, I thought. Maybe I slipped and maybe I didn't, but I nicked him slightly, so the blood rose up. He lost control and slapped me then—I saw the nowhere in his eyes and stiffened my neck like one of his Indians, left him staring, puzzled, at the red spot on his palm.

I touched my finger to the bead of blood and tasted it. His eyes softened, and went far away.

Here's what I want to do, he said.

It was as if he had persuaded me instead of forcing it, but then it often felt that way. I lay with knees up and my legs open, green calico dress bunched above my waist, looking up at the daddy longlegs walking over the rafters, the slow tremor of the snake skins. Terrell held the blade at both haft and tip, like a bone scraper, and worked with an entranced, extraordinary care.

In all the times we did this thing, he never cut me there. I never looked but I always pictured it, the clean white edge slipping over the soft curve of flesh, the astonishing sensation of cool steel. Now and then Terrell paused with the blade, moistened the ball of his thumb with his tongue to smooth away the little hairs he'd cut. I couldn't seem to stop myself (whatever self I had left then) from sighing as he stroked the new-smooth lobes . . . I bit my lip for a taste of my own blood. My brother kissed my blood away, snaked his tongue inside to claim it.

Sometimes, after such an afternoon there might be some careless, visible sign, a swollen lip or the fattening bruise on my jawbone where Terrell had been startled into striking me. Once in a while, the Mom-thing noticed things like that.

You play too rough, she'd say. And look at me.

28

Ursa Major clambered up the ink-black sky, casting cold light on the alkaline desert floor. I had walked a long way, far enough that the stains of city light had faded to sulfurous blooms on the horizon at my back. Ahead, the faint ribbon of a jackrabbit trail, packed to a just slightly paler shade than the loose sand surrounding it, wavered into a tumble of boulders that spilled down from the mesa there.

I crouched on my heels, beside a gnarl of juniper, clenching its dry roots into cracks of one great stone. The shadow of the bush fell over me, covering me with the dark.

High on the mesa, coyotes sang. The wild, high, half-hysterical crying sound. Sound carries strangely in the desert, so they might in fact have been miles away, and there might have been no more than a pair of them, though it sounded like a chorus of a dozen or more.

I watched for rabbits; there were none. Time passed, while overhead the stars kept turning, with that faint, scarcely audible music, as when you rub your spit-wet finger around the rim of a crystal glass.

The coyotes had stopped their concert long before. But now one came cautiously along the jackrabbit trail, out of the boulders, all covered with those clinging knots of juniper. Skulking, pausing often to hump up his back and turn his muzzle over his shoulder. Then with his ears rotating forward, pricked, he advanced again, with a spring in his step and a sharpening attention on the surface of the trail, though there was nothing to stalk that I could see, no rabbits, not a lizard, mouse or squirrel.

Maybe the coyote could see me in my hood of shadow. Maybe he could smell the blood, pumping the long circuit from my heart.

I stood up, clear of the shadow, making myself large. The coyote balked, cringing backward on folding knees, ears flat back to the fur of the head. His eyes pale globes of yellow, under the weak starlight.

Tonight I hadn't brought the rifle. The coyote and I remained in a frozen balance. Eventually I took a few slow backward steps; the coyote stayed right where he was.

I turned away and walked, not quickly, feeling a pale spot on my spine, though I knew very well a lone coyote would not attack a full-grown person, unless rabid, and this one showed no sign of that. Even that possibility was nothing to me.

Behind me, just possibly, a dry whisper of paws on the sand. When I looked back the coyote was still motionless.

Again. Next time I looked, the coyote's distance from the boulder might have changed a little. He was still.

Next time I looked I'd walked a mile or more and was near enough to the trailer park to pick out individual points of light from the blur. The coyote came loping after me now, but at a considerable distance on my back-trail.

I went on slowly, toward the artificial lights, thinking of how the first wild dogs must have come into camps, for whatever reason, to enslave themselves to men. When I reached the tear in the chain-link fence, the coyote was nowhere to be seen.

⟋ ⟋ ⟋

(o)

(o)

(o)

The open wound of emptiness . . .

⟋ ⟋ ⟋

Careless, I'd scraped my forearm going through the fence; blood beaded and absently I licked it clean as I climbed the wooden steps of my deck. The thick salt taste at the back of my throat. I wasn't hungry, thirsty, sleepy. There were still hours of night yet to pass.

I sprayed antiseptic on my arm; the sting of it barely seemed to reach me. Somehow the wireless phone was in my hand. For a second time I dialed the New York number.

"Hello . . ."

(o)

"Hello?"

Oh, I could certainly picture her then; I didn't need to watch the tape. On her knees with her head flung back, heavy breasts lifting through the cloth, crooked fingers clutching the sparkling dust-filled air.

"Mae," Laurel's voice burrowed in my ear. "Mae?"

I never gave her the penny, I thought. That was what I thought I wanted to say. But my lips were sealed, as if copper had been laid upon them, and my eyes were heavy under metal weight.

. . .

I didn't come to for a long time after, finally waking to scorched daylight, phone in my limp hand again, the robot voice advising me *if you would like to make a call* to hang it up.

29

I woke to the rattle of the bead curtain over Laurel's door. A dry wind from the desert shivered the strings. It died away and the beads fell still. I watched the light illuminating the colors of the glass. Early, but the heat was rising. Sweat glued the inside of my arm to Laurel's belly; I watched it rise and fall with the rhythm of her sleeping breath.

When I looked at her face again her eyes were open, though still blurred with sleep. She sat up suddenly, threw her hair back. Lifting the beads aside with the back of her wrist, she stood naked in the doorframe for a moment, looking out across the plain. Then she came in and fished out some clothes from the pile on the floor.

"Hot," Laurel said. I nodded.

I dressed myself, while Laurel packed her little metal hash pipe. We each took a hit and Laurel capped the pipe and kissed me, just on the edge of my lips; both of us had cotton mouth. She dug the water bottle out from a stale swirl of sheet, and held it to the light to show it empty.

We went to the lodge to get more water. D—— was

nowhere to be seen. Maybe he had gone to town, but none of the vehicles seemed to be missing. Two men leaned into the guts of one, holding a screwdriver and a wrench.

The sun, though scarcely risen, seemed to screw down on both of us like a clamp. A bad idea, maybe, to toke up so early in the morning. I'd drunk as much water as I could hold and still my mouth felt parched.

"Come on." Laurel smiled at me, with her chapped lips, and caught my hand. Her secret, knowing smile. "I know where we can go," she said.

I followed her down past Clive's cabin, through the collapsing Western set. A horned toad squatted on the steps of the saloon. Laurel made a feint at it, to make it hop, but the toad only blinked at her and inflated its slack gullet.

On the rise beyond the set, a trail wound past the big round rock, where D—— would sometimes assemble the People, to tell us his End Time stories. A crow perched there now, at the top of the boulder where D—— would sit cross-legged like a shaman or, when he became excited, caper in tight loops and brandish his fists. I had never been past that point, but Laurel seemed to know where she was going. A trail of sorts climbed through the piñon, over a fall of rocks. It was steep, and the tread of my sneakers was worn out, so sometimes I had to crouch and use my hands to get over the stones.

Laurel had pulled a pair of green flip-flops out of the

communal clothes heap in the lodge. One of the thongs tore loose as she climbed; she held it up with a disgusted look, then flung it away. It hung on a branch of a stunted pine, and Laurel went on barefoot, carrying the whole flip-flop in one hand.

Ahead of her I could see the bushy tops of oasis palms, springing up from a cleft in the ridge. I stopped a minute, and turned my face to the moist breeze that came from that direction. It was cooler now. When I looked back I could see stick figures moving around the lodge, way down below. The distant racket of a motor that had finally caught was like the whirring of an insect. The whole scene rippled in my sight, from a mixture of heat shimmer and hash.

When I caught up with Laurel, she had dropped the other flip-flop and was standing with her bare toes wrapped over the lip of a cliff. Twenty feet below, a blue pool was boiling with the water that rushed into it from three waterfalls, climbing in stair steps, right to left, up the face of the higher cliff on the other side. Here was where those palm trees grew, the fronds of them trembling, high above us. There was such a wealth of water that the froth of the falls spattered us with cool drops where we stood on the far side.

Laurel smiled, and touched the back of my hand with one finger. In two smooth motions she came out of her clothes, then threw herself down into the pool.

Over the roar of the falls, I couldn't even hear the splash. I hesitated before I followed, but Laurel seemed to know what she was doing, and now I could see the heads of another pair of swimmers moving in the water, near to hers.

I went down as deep as the space of empty air through which I'd fallen, but I never touched the bottom. At first it was so cold it made my back teeth hurt. There was a calm center down in the sapphire blue, like the opium core of the hash we had smoked. I opened my eyes underneath the water, and saw Laurel's bare legs swiveling like seaweed in the lens of distorted light at the surface. I kicked up and broke into the air beside her, gasping and laughing; Laurel was too.

I trod water, watching her swim. She did all her strokes correctly, like she'd learned at summer camp. I couldn't have matched her strength as a swimmer, but I didn't mind; it was pretty to see. After a little while she backstroked to the lowest fall and let the water shower over her upturned face. I paddled over to her, and rested on a shallow rock. Laurel came out of the water like a mermaid and sat on a wet stone with her legs folded under her. Her right breast lifted with the movement of her arm as she roped her hair back over one shoulder.

The other pair of swimmers had emerged on the other side of the pool from us. Though the rocks were surely slippery, they climbed surefooted and gracefully upright, until they reached a ledge below the middle fall. They turned in our direction then, although they didn't seem to know that we were there.

"Wow." Laurel touched a finger to her lower lip. "I think that's O——."

I recognized him then myself, from all the album covers and posters. O—— came around the ranch sometimes, I'd heard, but this was the first time I had seen him here. Supposedly D—— had lived for a while in O——'s house in Malibu, with some earlier configuration of the People, but that was before Laurel's time, or mine.

For me, O—— got his beauty from his music, but I could see Laurel was struck by his looks. And I suppose he was a handsome man, or boy, with the golden skin he got (some claimed) from a black father, the dark ringlets of his hair flattened down around his shoulders by the wet. But I was more impressed with Eerie on that morning; I don't think I have ever seen so beautiful a mortal body.

They were as unaware of us as if we'd been a couple of fish in the pool, but we did watch them, as they moved under the waterfall together. His gold hand slipped over her ivory hip to the small of her back, and they seemed to caress each other with skeins of the falling water. All their movements were so delicate, and marvelously slow. It felt as if their love rained down on me and Laurel, and watered all the places where we had been dry.

30

A fine gray dust blew over the desert. It coated every window, seeped in through every crack. All day the machines ate into the stone of the mountain. The incessant complaint of their alarms as they reversed and then returned to the attack. Between the clatter and the monotone came the whisper of pumps, sucking the aquifers dry. The endless racket of mortal engines, striving to build Babylon.

Gray dust caked in the back of my throat. I longed for my old voices, but heard nothing.

* * *

Raze it. Raze it. For the gods' sake, burn it down.

31

I went to Lake Mead, to look for water. The torpid surface stretched away, farther than the eye could see. There was the rush of the flumes in the sky-high dam, the chatter of tourists, and the cries of gulls circling overhead, a thousand miles away from the sea, dipping and diving to snatch at our leavings.

A casino for scavengers. The gulls flew down with the devotion of marks milking the handles of slot machines. I saw one swoop to snatch a whole sandwich, beak lashing over the shoulder of a tourist's child. The father shook his fist and gave chase as the bread and meat scattered over the boardwalk and other gulls swooped down to claim their portion.

When the tourists cast their bread upon the waters, the dull lake's surface boiled with the rubbery lips of carp, struggling with one another over every soggy crumb.

As I left, a beggar accosted me. I shrugged him off without looking, but somehow took him in all the same. Out of his scabby face, his eyes probed toward me. His grubby hand kept reaching. Somehow he seemed to know my name.

When I took a second look, it was Corey. I couldn't count the days since he'd been fired from the casino, but it could hardly have been so many, for him to have plummeted so far. I gave him a handful of change from my pocket and walked on.

32

"Mae," Laurel said, the next time I called, and after a moment I answered her. A little spring opened up in me when I pronounced her name.

And then, I think, we must have had a conversation. Or, at any rate, Laurel began to talk. *It's been so long . . .* banalities of that order. For the first few minutes I listened only to the timbre of her voice.

Laurel had been to a New England prep school, then a couple of years at Stanford before she fell in with D—— and the People. Her patrician manner of speaking probably came from her family, long before any of those other things had occurred. I'd envied that a little, I suppose, in the beginning. But in her passion Laurel spoke differently; her register dropped; the voice took on richer tones. I heard the wildness that was in her, raging to come out.

Then. I heard that then. Tonight, she gave me only her schooled surface, and I said little: *Yes . . . Go on . . .* I let the silence pool whenever she stopped speaking.

Without attending to her words, I somehow gleaned

some information. Laurel had moved to New York, where she taught school. She was some stripe of administrator now, in a top-drawer prep school in Greenwich Village. Yes, she was single still, or again. But there was a child, a daughter—I didn't catch her name.

Beneath the careful modulation of her voice I heard nothing of her old fire, but an uneasiness. A hint of fear. It repulsed me and drew me toward it.

"Laurel," I said. "I saw you."

"You—"

"The tapes." I didn't mean to say tapes, that I had made them, that I had watched her seven seconds on the order of seven hours. I meant to say the television.

"In the news," I said.

Laurel held her breath and I pictured her pinning her plump lower lip in her top teeth as she masked the telephone's mouthpiece with her hand.

"The nine-eleven coverage."

"Oh *God*." A deeper shade came into her voice, though she wasn't calling on the gods that she and I had served. "I've so been trying to forget that. That—it wasn't me."

I no longer needed to play the tape to see it, Laurel with her head thrown back, clawing hands raised against heaven, her bloody jaws. Laurel translated into Fury, the blazing self she was meant to be.

"I don't see how you *saw* that, Mae." She was struggling to repair the seamless surface of her speech. "They only played it a few times." A shudder I could feel across the phone line. "A time too many for me, of course."

Silence.

"It's been hard here. It's . . . it's all such desolation."

"I live in the desert," I told her, the first and only circumstance of that nature I revealed.

"I don't see how you found me, anyway. After so long."

The fear was there again beneath the surface and I wanted to move through my disgust into it, occupy it, and use the fear to hurt her, or rather to make her feel.

There's a bond between us, never broken. I never lost you, Laurel, and no more could you lose me.

For the first time on the phone, she sounded old. "I can't do this, Mae. I just can't handle it. I don't know what you want from me anyway. Not now. What is there? And besides—"

Besides.

"I'm dying," Laurel said into the phone.

"You can't be."

"Yes I can," she blurted out. Her voice shifted to irritability, still only on the surface at first. Then something deeper; I thought she might weep. "Mae, I don't know where you are, but I can't go back into that crazy fantasy with you. I can be dying like anyone else, and I am."

It upset me, I am ashamed to say. Laurel, saying a

thing like that. It pushed me off my center for a moment, and made me start to plead.

"Don't you remember . . . ?"

"Can't you understand I don't *want* to remember?" The voice moved from petulant to firm; I felt her hardening her shell. "Mae, I wish you well, but please don't call."

✦ ✦ ✦

In the desert there was starlight but no moon. The dust had settled, for a time, and the air was calm and dry. I heard coyotes, not so far away, but didn't see them.

Reach out and touch someone, I thought. I hadn't yet considered that someone could touch you back.

33

What if, with Laurel, it had never been enough? The prospect of tenderness endlessly unfolding, pleasure without pain—like meat without salt. It left, untended, the desire to be stabbed in the heart.

So then one day. So then.

· · ·

O—— appeared at the lodge and asked if I'd seen Eerie. He was fretful, gold skin crimped between his brows. Barefoot, shirtless, he got out of his rock-star convertible, and cast about the grounds before coming toward me. No one else was in sight. Well, there was one of those bikers who liked to hang around the place, tinkering with a dune buggy engine, but all you could see of him was his raggedy gang colors humped over the open hood, the crack of his ass poking out of his jeans.

"Not here," I told him, which was technically true, depending on your definition of *here*. As a matter of fact I knew just where Eerie was—in the school-bus wing stroked out on the smack Ned had given her—but she wasn't in the lodge and I could prove it. And if O——

was worried that Eerie might be with D——, I knew that she wasn't, because someone else was.

I caught O——'s hand, trying for the flower-girl carelessness that Laurel would have used to make that move. But O—— seemed to pull away from the touch, so I let him go and merely beckoned him inside.

"Come on," I said. Inside the lodge, I showed him all the places Eerie was not, which included D——'s octagon room up top. A flowered sheet hung across the doorway at the head of the stairs, quivering slightly with a breeze coming in from the other side. I stopped to listen but heard nothing, then pulled a ripple of sheet back.

"Don't let him see you," I whispered into O——'s ear. Not that D—— would have cared who saw him do what—but if he knew that O—— was present he would have bent his energy on keeping him there and using him for something.

I must have already plotted what I would do next, if I didn't want that to happen.

However, D—— was asleep, or feigning sleep, or turned deeply inward—the blind mask covering his face with empty eyeholes streaming backward to the stars . . . Or one might have said his shut-eyed face was peaceful, even beatific. The back of his hand lay on Laurel's bare belly, just above the first cinnamon crinkle of the hair between her legs, rising and easily falling with her sleeping breath.

I waited near the foot of the stairs till O—— let the

sheet fall back into place and came down, relieved, to join me. But I didn't try for his hand again. I'd need to do it my way and not Laurel's.

You're the knife and I'm the butter.

I stepped within O———'s compass and smiled up at him; he didn't move away this time. O——— was tall, a clear head taller than me, so I had to tilt my head to catch his eye.

"See?" I began. "It's—"

There was a code word then that covered everything. It expressed that actions had no consequences, that we could all do whatever we pleased, you go your way and I go mine and if we chance to meet it's beautiful . . . Here in the twenty-first century *it's cool* covers all that sort of business, but back then . . .

"Out of sight," I said to O———, and apparently those were the perfect words to make him reach for me.

34

When it was over, nearly over, there was a baby still alive, in the belly of one of the dead women there on the floor of the house in the canyon. I knew because I saw it move. And I remembered Semele, her mortal body immolated in the fire and the light of Zeus. How the god took fetal Dionysus from the charred flesh of his dead lover and sewed him into his own thigh, till the time was ripe for a second bearing.

I wanted to go back to take the baby, have it, release it, bring it to bear. But by then we were leaving, hurrying now—when I turned back the others caught my upper arms and hustled me away.

35

Mary-Alice was her name and she was a cheerleader, though not the one the sports fans looked at most; she was shorter than the rest, and chunkier, which was revealed when she leaped into the air squealing and shivering her pompoms, and the maroon pleats of her skirt swung out to flash the yellow satin underpants. When not cheerleading she liked to wear white blouses just a little too tight, a dear little roll of pudge at her waistband and the ghost of a sweat stain under her arm, all through those suffocating days of early fall. Her little pink nose turned up like a pig's, and a small gilt crucifix hung in the hollow of her throat, which, I admit, I sometimes thought of slashing.

The Mom-thing was pleased that Terrell was finally *dating*—pleased and relieved and, when she looked at me, triumphant, it appeared. She cut at me with her smug regard, huffing out smoke from her two nostrils, her whole head a bundle of curlers wrapped in a frizzy polyester kerchief—shooting the look toward me through the smudged cat's-eye glasses, leashed to her skinny neck with a beaded chain.

So I went out and let the screen door bang, the whine of the spring and the whine of her voice behind me. Through the haze of autumn heat, the window above the garage seemed to shimmer, wrapped in vine like Ouroboros strangling, hatching its egg. What he'd want that she could give him, I couldn't very well conceive.

He took her to the movies, to the Pullman diner for burgers and shakes. They were making plans to go to the prom, when it was still eight months away, and by God, he even went to church with her family! . . . though that was only a time or two; he didn't make it a habit. Then he started taking her parking at night, up into the woods to the dead-end turnarounds of the unfinished subdivision, at the edge of where it was still wild back there.

He left me, then, to my own devices—which he and I had been at pains for me to master.

To be sure, there were others than my brother, beginning with his comrades on the swim team. Somewhat to my own surprise at first, I discovered I had what it took to work my way through a number of these. There was nothing to it, really; nothing in it. Even the ones who liked to play tough, or the ones with some veneer of real meanness—once I punched through the crust there was nothing much but jelly inside.

Unlike my brother, those other boys didn't know the value of a secret—as if whatever I did with them could have a secret value. So presently girls in the school hallways began to nudge one another and shoot me cutting glances, like the ones I got from the Mom-thing at home.

I didn't listen to those living whispers. I heard spectral voices, across the aeons, calling me by my name. If anything ever got back to Terrell, he gave me no sign.

36

I took the rifle into the desert and waited by the rabbit trail, crouched in the shadow of a boulder. No rabbits. No water. In my dry mouth I held a stone.

I could hear mice moving but I couldn't see them, which was strange when the color of night was so pale. There was a moon, and the desert floor curved away from its sere light, like a moonscape reflected. Dark spines of yucca probed out of the cracks among white rocks. Toward the horizon, a switch of broom grass and the twisted branches of mesquite reaching wraithlike into the sky.

A scent of the smoke of blood sacrifice, rising between the horns of the altar. Horns of the moon.

. . .

Presently a coyote came, hunting mice—quick and alert as a cat, fixing invisible prey with his eyes and then pouncing. I raised the rifle and found him in the scope. The coyote turned his head toward me. Ears up, poised. All his being focused on the shadow of the rock where surely he must know I was.

We balanced there, for a long time. I held him in the crosshairs until dawn, and let him go.

37

The next time I saw O——

    . . . I mean after our fling to Malibu, which I had never expected to last long. It was like when you pick up a stray cat and play with it a little while and then forget it, let it go. It doesn't probably occur to you that the little cat could have rabies.

When I was small Terrell taught me how to catch snakes and keep them—not the poison snakes, of course, but chicken snakes and the black snakes that the summer woods were full of. They'd get used to you after a while and twine around your arms and legs, warming to the temperature of the blood inside your body. We kept them in a basket, till hunger turned them mean again, but often they could go a week before that happened.

I hadn't expected more from my escapade with O——. No woman of the People could come up to Eerie. I knew I was there for a distraction and that was fine with me. I think I honestly hoped to make him feel a little better, if only for a time. And with Laurel called away, to D——'s panopticon atop the lodge, what else was I supposed to do?

I stopped to wonder, what could be D——'s purpose? If down in the dark hollows of the god mask, D—— had known that I would go, or even somehow pointed me in that direction. But I never thought of that for long, because I was still with O—— in Malibu, and it was sweet.

The house was right there on the beach, like a white block castle, ultramodern with lots of glass and stupendous views. Every morning somebody would bring us fresh-squeezed orange juice and usually we'd go out to swim, shouting and diving after each other in the surf. O—— had to teach me some of that, because I still wasn't used to the ocean.

There were plenty of other people around, some of them staying in the house, and I never knew for sure how many or where exactly it was that they slept. Beautiful People. Small packs of groupie women floated in and out, sometimes high-fashion types, sometimes more exotic hippie chicks or genuine foreigners, wreathed in a funk of patchouli and the henna tattoos that curled over their hands and their feet.

O—— paid no more attention to them than he would to flowers, or not while I was here. I suppose if you get all you want you finally have too many. But fucking, *balling* O—— was nothing special, despite my skills. Of course I'd known from the beginning he wasn't really there for me.

Then there were musicians, good ones all, who came to play with O———, who had a room, a kind of studio, I think, with lots of guitars and amps, a drum set, with a big glass wall overlooking the sea. But I liked best to hear him play and sing alone, in the evenings with the sun going down red and gold across the strand and the surf—O——— would play one of his big honey-colored acoustics and I would (I did this) curl up at his feet. Then the voices in my head would stop and I heard nothing but the vast annealing resonance of O———'s voice.

The words—I didn't really hear them. Most of those songs went onto the album *Western Wind*. They tended to be sad songs in minor keys, of love and loss and with a spell to charm the return of the lost lover.

Then one day, O——— didn't want me in the music room anymore. He was looking over my shoulder when he told me that, to someplace way out in the Pacific, like Hawaii, maybe. That's when I learned how perfectly soundproof that room really was. Outside on the terrace I watched through the glass, his mouth and his hands silently swimming . . . Surf sounds in my ears behind me, dark hollow forming again in my head. So I knew that O——— was singing for Eerie, not for me.

, , ,

I wondered then if he could have found out, if O——— *knew* that I knew that Eerie was there when he came looking for her. Maybe, maybe not, but not long after I left Malibu O——— came out to the ranch again, and I knew he wouldn't be looking for me.

It was night, this time, and the first we heard of it was a shout and scuffle. Laurel and I were in her room, and the racket came from farther down the gangplank— Ned's voice raised, and a voice not recognizable as O———'s, with that harsh tone of anger. We pulled on our clothes and went to check it out.

As Laurel and I arrived on the scene, O——— pushed Ned in the center of his chest again and Ned faked a fall backward, to a soft landing on his mattress, wings of his black vest flying open and the silver ankh flopping on his breastbone. He didn't try to get up, but displayed the V sign with both hands.

"Peace, man, *peace!*" Ned panted. "Don't *freak out,* man."

O——— glowered down on him from the doorway, and between them Eerie sat quietly crying, her whole head hidden in her hair.

"Like *you* know anything about peace," O——— said. "Like you care."

Laurel opened her mouth to say something but I stopped her. *Let it happen,* I thought, or maybe said. It was curious that D———, who had the most sensitive nose for trouble, hadn't appeared to settle this problem. Maybe he wasn't on the premises, or maybe he was deliberately sitting it out.

"Listen, man," Ned started again. "Do you think you own her? It's a free—"

"Shut the fuck up!" O—— snapped at him. "I'm not talking to you."

I didn't think he'd have a lot of luck talking to Eerie. Even with her head clutched in both hands like that I could see the railroad running up her forearms, and I remembered from my days with Louie: when a girl gets that far gone she can hear dope talking but not much more.

O—— didn't talk to her. He sang. Or he was singing—neither Laurel nor I heard how he began. Somehow too he had produced an instrument and was playing. Were there words? There must have been words. It was as if his fingers strummed upon our viscera. Out of his mouth came a golden orb of light.

Eerie lifted her head and looked at him. She smoothed all her hair toward the back of her head. Her tears were drying on her cheeks. Though her skin had shrunk to the bone of her skull, her beauty was still frightening. I understood that the song of O—— was infusing her with energy—the strength to stand. To move toward him.

No one attended to Ned's muttering: *lethergothenshe's-freetogoI'mnotstoppingherifshewantstoleave* . . .

I saw then how O—— and Eerie were embraced in spirit, though their bodies did not touch. When she came near, O—— smiled and turned out through the doorway, still drawing her along, delicately but definitely, at a certain magnetic distance. Laurel and I parted to let them pass. O——'s song still radiated from his lips. He stepped down from the gangplank into the dark, with Eerie following him.

A little shimmer of jealousy rang between me and Laurel, when O—— and Eerie walked between us. Then it passed and we turned our heads together in the direction they had gone.

Behind us, Ned was snickering, louder now. *Don't look back!*

That night was overcast, and pitch-black, so when they stepped off the gangway, they might as well have fallen into outer space. We could see nothing, only the shining of the song of O——, diminishing to a pinpoint in the darkness. He must have parked his car a long way off. I could just make out some other witnesses, those who happened to wear light garments, still as tombstones, pale as shades. So none of us saw if O—— looked back or not.

38

Crunchy and Creamy made tea in the lodge, and all the People assembled to drink it. How did we all know to go there?

I had a pulse in the back of my head, the soft dark spot where tendon meets bone, that roused me from where I lay with Laurel, like a pair of lizards waiting out the afternoon heat. And I caught Laurel's fingertips to bring her along, although I let go of her hand before we had gone far. Not so much to hide that touch from D——, who knew all about it anyway, but.

The People moved toward the lodge from various directions, drawn perhaps by the funky aroma of the tea. Or maybe it was the pull of D——'s intention. We could feel it, one could feel it, like a lodestone. The smell was stronger the nearer you got.

With a certain solemnity, Crunchy and Creamy ladled from their cauldron into Styrofoam cups. The tea was black and tasted smoky, musty. I must have been very distracted that day, because it wasn't till my vision started to go strange around the edges that I knew we'd just been drinking psilocybin, and the People were all going off on a higgledy-piggledy trip.

D—— came downstairs then, wearing a blue-flowered kimono so much too long for him that the hem trailed behind like a bridal gown's train. I thought he wore lipstick and painted nails but that might have been just an effect of the drug. He stitched himself through the People like a minnow through water. Here a touch, there a kiss. There a whisper. We were thirty or forty strong that day. Girls mostly, but a double handful of men. But some of the men were just there for the party.

D——'s voice began, rapt, sonorous. The voice didn't seem to come out of his throat. It surrounded his whole body, like an aura. That might have been an effect of the drug.

It's all starting to come down, the voice said.

D—— began undressing Stitch, loosening the white buttons on her pale blue work-shirt—same shirt as Creamy and Crunchy wore under their vests. Stitch stood as passively as a child, except that in her smile I saw the points of her teeth.

Oh, yeah. The voice. *We'll break it down.*

Like most of the women of the People (Laurel being a great blowsy exception to this rule), Stitch had a boyish build, next to nothing in hips and breasts—and yet her body was very well made. A sigh went all around the lodge when D—— had laid it bare.

O

O

The drug made it a yawning hollow, echoing, deep. Stitch tossed back her dirty hair, exposing her white throat. Soundlessly she sank down to her knees before him. But D—— connected her to another and moved on.

The voice. *Me.*

At the fringes of my vision there began to be little cobwebs of op-art graphics. Not possible for me to blink them away. The drug, taking me into itself regardless of my will. Without further prompting, others, everyone, began to disrobe. I looked away from Laurel. The other way from her. A disposable person behind me assisted me with my clothes. It had taken him only a second to shed the ridiculous striped djellaba he always wore. So I must know him, though I didn't know his name. Was he one of the People or just . . . there. For the ride. With Jesus hair like all the rest, but melting brown eyes like a puppy's. A pulsing psychedelic cobweb crawled over the left side of his face. I looked away. D——'s hands assisted our connection.

Me. Me.

D——'s kimono had disappeared. He was half erect in that cloud of goat hair but otherwise only a certain tightness in his voice betrayed any sort of erotic involvement. He didn't participate, directly. He conducted.

Guiding, encouraging. Inserting. For the more difficult connections he had a prosaic little tube of KY jelly.

Memememememe . . .

The mushrooms turned it into a sort of cricket sound as I sank deeper. Bonelessly bending. All the sounds warped. D—— bent people to his plan. Like Gumby. What was the name of Gumby's horse? The various noises of suction began to grow unbearably loud. That familiar sensation: the invasion of arousal. Willing or no.

Let go of me. Let go of mememe . . .

I agreed, I suppose. Or there was no longer an *I* to agree. Or suppose. A butterfly shutter wheeled over my vision. Darkness. Darkness. Light. More darkness. When it opened I saw or perceived that the People were linked into one great wriggling wreath around the central fireplace, which was cold and smelled of ancient ash. When it closed I saw eyelid movies of Day-Glo green and yellow fields, goats prancing, a woman turning into reeds.

My People. Be One. Be One.

A reduplicated compound. A beast of many backs. It hunched. It moaned.

Let go of meme. Higgledy-piggledy—let it all come down. Be One.

I was then unpleasantly penetrated by the thought that although Laurel was several places away in this vast fucking daisy chain, I was still most tangibly connected to her, through the transitive power of fucking. At the repulsion of this idea I groaned, which encouraged the beast, when I had no wish to encourage it. I could find no voice to say to Laurel that I really didn't care a damn for O——, that I had gone off with him only to hurt her. There was only one voice in the bowels of the beast and the voice seemed only to speak to *mememe* though I knew it was meant for all the One People.

Hung up on each other. Hung up on yourselves. You can't hear the gods' great voices. You're too busy—talking to yourselves.

In the midst of it all there was mere discomfort. Skin scraped across the splintery floor.

Can't you hear the gods' great voices—

The truth came through D——. Was not of him. Perhaps D—— didn't himself understand it. Except for the special times when he did.

I wanted to say *I hear them, I do! I hear gods' voices. The words they shape around me like a door.* But I couldn't, not only because some fleshy thing had stopped my throat.

I knew this bacchanalia was not what I had come for. This was not the bacchanalia I had come for. That was elsewhere. My frenzy. One's frenzy. I knew that it had happened before, if I and I only heard the true voices, and I knew it was going to happen again.

39

Pauley's rifle came in a long rectangular case like a guitar, with plush-lined compartments for the rifle itself and for the scope and the Starlite attachment and for the silencer, a big awkward thing, the size of a wine bottle. Out in the desert there was no one to hear, but one night I took the silencer with me, just the same.

It didn't weigh a quarter as much as a wine bottle, but it did change the balance of the weapon. I practiced till I'd adjusted to the difference, finding targets but not firing. A point of stone or a fallen branch. Things already dead. That never lived.

. . .

To reach out with an invisible silent fatal touch . . .

. . .

Then, movement. In the scope a flicker of phosphorescent green. With the silencer the shot made scarcely any more sound than a sneeze, or the sound of someone spitting on dry sand. I *made* myself prop the rifle carefully upright against a stone before I fell on the coyote, my blade drawn. Coyote still kicking spasmodically, scuffing fine gravel with his claws. The dead jaws snapping.

Gutted it. Skinned it. As Terrell had taught me all those years ago, when we used to go out together to hunt deer. The knife I had now was not the best I had ever owned, and was getting dull by the time I got to the difficult part. I sharpened it against a stone, resumed the flaying. At last the head skin came off whole. I stopped, on my knees, propped up on my palms, panting like a dog.

Blood to my elbows. In the weak starlight, against the pale floor of the desert, it looked black. The sound of my breath like a rasp on dry wood.

I stood up slowly, raising the limp skin by its shoulders, and looked into the vacant eyeholes of the god mask. Presence in absence. The unavoidable fixed stare. If the features seemed to shiver it must have been because my hands were slightly trembling. The smile now curling fondly at the corners, peeled from its blood-stained teeth, which lay near me on the ground. At my feet the carcass was now still, wronged and irreparable, leaching its sticky fluids into the sand.

Facing the hum of light pollution on the horizon, I raised the skin above my head. Rank smell of musk and blood surrounding me now. Limp mask dangling before my face. I did not want the skin to touch me this time, to settle on my shoulders like a mantle. Awkwardly I held it up, over and away from me, balancing and aligning. To look back, through the eyes of the beast, at the dying glow of the mortal world.

40

Again, again I gazed at Laurel, on her knees, her crooked hands clawing at the sky. The bared throat and blind head tossing. *Αγωνία. Έκσταση*. The place where pain and pleasure are one.

Just suffer, I said, inside my mind. *Don't try to make anything of your suffering.*

Was I talking to Laurel, or myself, or to O——? There was a point where I differed from them. That had been O——'s big mistake, to believe that suffering could be redeemed, instead of polluted, by such a transformation.

41

I came to myself sitting on the deck. Cold phone cupped between my hands. Worn out with complaint, the battery had died.

How many times I must have called. Over and over, hour on hour. But never, not once, another answer.

I could picture the phone ringing in her place. Or maybe it rang only in my ear, if she had switched it off. Or maybe she sat there and watched it ring. It couldn't be true, her claim that she was dying.

First light. On the horizon, a circling of black wings, where carrion birds had found the carcass. The empty skin where I'd left it, shriveled to the stones.

42

At loose ends, with Terrell out on a *date,* I took his pipe and the bayonet and went into the woods. Once the houselights had disappeared behind me I stopped and fired a bowl of the cheap green Mexican that was everywhere in those days. Then I went on along the deer trails, the metal of the little pipe contracting as it cooled in the front pocket of my cut-off jeans.

In ten or fifteen minutes, I could see better in the dark. By then I was climbing higher on the ridge, through stands of oak and maple trees whose leaves had mostly fallen now. I had brought the bayonet along because I found it comforting and who knew what you might meet in the woods? It was deer season too, and the thought popped into my mind that maybe it was unwise to be walking those trails in the dark, in the nondescript colorless clothing I wore.

I stopped, scanned the hillside with my dilated pupils; the scene appeared almost as bright as day. I was trying to swallow my unease when I heard the *crump* of a heavy rifle firing, not at all far off. And nearer to me still, across a leaf-filled gulley that ran water in wet weather, a grunt and a speckled thrashing on the opposite slope.

I ran for a clearing, a pale space nearby. Burst out panting into one of those hillside turnarounds, where construction had stopped for the season or for want of funds. Down in the valley a single earthmover still crouched motionless, like the skeleton of a dinosaur. Much of the thin coat of gravel had been washed out or worn away and the red mud was rutted by the tracked equipment or by the tires of vehicles like Terrell's truck, parked now at the edge of the flat gray griddle of the turnaround, throbbing gently there.

That must surely have been a trick of my stoned eyes, but it got worse. It wasn't just movement but also sound; not only squeaking on its elderly shocks, the truck was whimpering like a live thing . . . It took me a long rubbery time to construct the idea that Terrell must have spread a camp mat on the truck bed. Spread Mary-Alice on the mat . . .

I ran back into the woods with the bayonet thrust out before me, gripped in my two hands, as if I were charging some enemy battle line. My mouth was wide open but I don't think I was screaming—dark air rushed into me, not out. I stumbled in the gully, and got wet all the way up my bare shins; under the surface of dry leaves was a foot of water and rot and muck—I slowed down then, abruptly conscious of the risk I'd impale myself if I tripped and fell with what I carried.

The hunter had abandoned the dead fawn, because it was too little to be legal, or maybe because he was too poor a tracker to find it in the first place. So young that it still had its spots. That seems impossible to me now—it would have been too late in the season—but at the time that's what I saw.

 * * *

A red haze came swimming over my vision, throwing out tentacles like a squid.

 * * *

. . . and the next thing I saw, remember seeing, was Mary-Alice popping upright, covering her breasts with her pudgy white hands, gaping and gasping, her eyes going wide. Flung from her, Terrell knocked his head on the wall of the truck bed, old metal ringing back like a dull school bell.

Before the two of them I stood revealed, barefoot and bloody, naked but for raw fawnskin, my pine-branch thyrsus wreathed in poison ivy or crawling with snakes for all I know. My shoes were gone, my clothes I never found again, nor the little pipe in the jeans pocket, but I must have hung on to the bayonet, because I found it again later, among Terrell's things.

Presently Mary-Alice began to scream, on an automatic clockwork rhythm. She went on screaming like a little dog yaps, the kind of dog that doesn't know why it's barking, may not even know that it *is* barking.

What did Terrell do then? I don't remember. I have no image in my mind.

◆ ◆ ◆

Then, more red haze. My vision flickering. In the clear spots there are certain pictures. Bare bloody footprints across the curling linoleum of the kitchen floor . . . from the front room, the crackle of the television, funk of cigarette smoke and Sanka, querulous sound of Dad and the Mom-thing bickering, or the Mom-thing bickering all by herself . . . I picture her brandishing the fawnskin at me, shrieking or making the motions of shrieking. Her black mouth round and silent as a lamprey's . . .

But that must have been days or even weeks later, when she found the skin crumpled under the bed or in a corner of the closet, after it had begun to smell. If indeed it happened at all, for I no longer seem to know if all these things really did occur, or if I dreamed them.

43

I got out my old copy of *Western Wind* again, and opened it up to look at the pictures. It was sad how everyone appeared to be so young. Though we'd managed to make O——'s youth eternal. Thanks to our devotion, everyone would always see him in the high bloom of his prime.

The songs were all about Eerie, I knew, but she couldn't have been there when those pictures were taken. O—— had led her from Ned's room directly to— they didn't call it "rehab" in those days. Too discreet to have a word for them, such places surely did exist, secluded gardens full of orange juice and sunshine. And rubber rooms, because I seem to know that Eerie had to kick cold turkey, banging her head against walls and floor . . .

I sat back from the album cover, pressing my fingers on closed eyelids—yes, Laurel had gone on a detour for a week or so around that time—*detour* was what she liked to call them. Laurel still got money from home and unlike the other members of the People she had enough of an undissolved ego to keep most of her money out of

D——'s reach. So if she needed to go on a detour once in a while, she didn't have to do it as a beggar.

These little sequences of events purled through my brain like beads on a string. What did they matter? There was no cause in them that could bind an effect, and yet I seemed to know quite clearly that Laurel had dropped out of sight for a spell sometime after that day of mushroom tea and D——'s daisy chain—Laurel often needed a good detour after one of those sessions, which did make it hard for any two individuals to be comfortable with each other in the way that they had been before. Hard to be at ease in your own skin. That was the point of the exercise, in fact, as D—— would be happy to explain to anyone whenever.

So Laurel had quietly abstracted a small sum of time from the sum she had dedicated to the People and to D——, and gone off with it somewhere all on her own . . . and Laurel had a marvelous gift for making her most calculated moves look like air-headed, mute and helpless accidents. So she might have—almost certainly had—simply stuck a couple of flowers in her hair and turned up on O——'s doorstep in Malibu, or more likely happened to run into him while frolicking, fairy-like, on the beach.

Of course she'd have known she was only a stand-in (as I had known it during my sojourn) when O—— sang his songs for Eerie to her. I don't suppose it bothered her, really. Laurel was a practical girl in a number of ways, so she'd have known that she was getting all she could. When I looked at her foot on the album cover I could picture as well her satisfied smile, just beyond the photographer's frame. And I knew that foot most intimately, not only the toe ring and the vinous swirls of henna but its every muscle, tendon, and bone.

Could Laurel have had the influence to get the rest of her cropped from the shot? No, I don't think so. It was only that the photographer was more interested in O——...

... who should have been looking only at Eerie. Who should never have taken his eyes off Eerie. For he did love her like no other, if he learned it only when it was too late.

44

In the winter Terrell began picking up Mary-Alice to take her to school with us, and even in springtime this habit continued. Still half asleep or pretending to be, I got out when we pulled into her driveway, staring dazedly at the cement Saint Francis on the lawn, tilting between their rock garden and a murky tarnished fish pool. Her mother waving cheerily from the doorstep or the window.

Mary-Alice climbed daintily to the middle of the bench seat and, when I got in behind her, made her snuggling into Terrell seem more like shrinking away from me. Maybe it was because of the talk in the halls—or that peculiar night in the woods (if she hadn't managed to shriek all memory of that away). Or maybe Mary-Alice was aware of something different, something other . . . In any case, she drew her skirt away, she shrank, avoiding all contact.

Until that morning when she turned from him and threw herself across my lap, so that, I realized after the first astonished second, she could vomit out the open window on my side. Terrell pulled over, with a half smile of puzzlement, a ghost of concern for her discomfort. Mary-Alice didn't drink (she'd hold a rum and Coke at a party, now and then wetting her tongue in it like a kitten), and she didn't get high, so it wouldn't be the aftermath of partying too hearty.

She was wearing a fuzzy angora sweater, pink with white buttons, and through it I could feel her soft torso limp against me, like a fallen soufflé. I could feel her heartbeat and her fear. Her heart was going as fast as a rabbit's. A few droplets of bile clung to the long pink hairs of the sweater.

Terrell asked if she was all right. If he should turn around and take her back home. Terrell gave her a stick of gum. Dentyne, I think. Terrell took fanatical care of his teeth and believed Dentyne to aid in that mission. Mary-Alice blinked her wet eyes and said, no, no, that she was fine . . . Terrell smiled, shrugged, put the truck on the road. So far, he had no idea.

◆ ◆ ◆

But the rest of the reel went by very quickly. A good Catholic girl. A whole Catholic *family*. So of course there was no question of— The Mom-thing biting her lip as she smoked. Dad seemed to take it rather more leniently. They weren't the first couple to get started early. When life comes your way you ought to accept it. A priest or a pastor must have furnished that line.

Mary-Alice wasn't showing a bit, but she sat demurely on the edge of her seat, eyes downcast and her soft hands cradling her navel, like a prim little pink-and-white Madonna. While Terrell looked around the room with the eyes of a wolf in a trap.

Small hurried wedding, *intimate,* one might have said—just the two families, and those not complete. The Catholic Church—the Romans, as we called them then. Did they burn incense? Not in our little town. But I can still picture the Mom-thing bridling as the priest murmured Latin, as though she were a witch being exorcised.

I have to imagine all that part, because I wasn't there. And Terrell himself was barely there, though no one yet knew he'd already enlisted, would be hustled off to boot camp in a matter of days. Then over to Nam. Somebody, everybody else, would get left holding the baby.

Not me. I stripped Dad's wallet and the Mom-thing's purse, then climbed into the garage attic room. Just a few lengths ahead of Mom's certain arrival, armed with doilies and ruffled curtains, vacuum and Lysol. I inhaled a last whiff of the close dark smell of smoke and rot, old blood, and dried spunk. But I wasn't there for sentimental reasons. I took the two packs of Newports and the half-pint of whiskey and the half-ounce of pot and the bayonet and our stone knife too, because I wanted to be sure to leave him nothing.

Nothing at all of what we once had. I had lived for sixteen years and my brother had been fucking me for five of them. I hitched downtown, to the corner where the Greyhound stopped, by the bank, and bought myself a ticket to the Summer of Love.

45

I turned back once I'd slipped through the tear in the fence behind my trailer, and looked again across the desert. Pale glow of dawn on the white flats and a low wind tumbling the weeds. On the horizon I seemed to see the figure of a person, no bigger than a matchstick in my eyes, unusually and so effortlessly lithe and erect that he was clearly not a member of our kind. Framed in the chain-link diamond I peered through, he seemed to hold an arrow, or perhaps a spear. I felt then he must have come to announce something to me. Something.

I strained my ears, heard nothing. The windblown cry of a bird. Flittering, diminishing. The black-throated sparrow, possibly. *Zacatonero garganta negra.* I don't know all the voices of the desert birds.

A grumble of machinery in the mountains to the east, grinding, powdering. The line between the ragged ridge-top and the sky glowed incandescent red, increasing its intensity. Burning. That figure on the horizon now no more than a vertical dark line. Lost when the sunrise finally spilled over and poured its red gold light all over the white barren like a bloodstain.

46

I want you to go with so-and-so, D——— would tell a girl sometimes. *Go with Bobby Bo,* or *Go with Long-John Larry.* (There were girls who liked to go with Long-John Larry, who didn't have that nickname for no reason.) *Go with* meant to let the guy have you for . . . as long as he wanted, in any and every way he wanted.

There were a couple of half-derelict motels up on the highway that the guys could use for this purpose—and D——— often preferred they leave the ranch, if hard drugs were going to be involved. Eerie was found dead in one of those. And Ned had furnished a cave up on the dry ridge—a laborious walk, and well out of earshot of the buildings, though just a short hop in one of the dune buggies, supposing any of them were running. He might let the other guys use it, depending. Most girls didn't like to go with Ned.

One went, however, if One was asked to go.

Ned liked to watch things suffer. He liked to pull the legs off bugs. He could spend a whole afternoon shooting horned toads in their loose bellies with a pellet pistol, watching their fluids leak out on the sand, perusing them for symptoms of sensation. In his flat green eyes the same neutral curiosity as when he'd wire up a new room or tinker with a motor.

Ned was a mortal, a bondsman of death, and even his cruelty was shallow, like his eyes.

D—— wanted me to go with Ned one time . . . the time that Laurel was away with O——, I think. I know. I didn't refuse, exactly, but somehow it didn't happen.

D——, Ned, and I were standing in . . . some space somewhere. On three vertices of a triangle with the dry air crackling between us. *Trust me,* I thought, *you wouldn't enjoy it.* I didn't have the bayonet, but I ran my thumb along the air where the edge of it would have been.

It wasn't that I had no taste for pain. I just didn't have any taste for Ned. If you needed something fixed he was fine, but after that forget it.

Ned went slack and dropped the subject. Wandered off. Then again, taking Laurel to the cave was probably an even better way of hurting me.

D——'s reasons were—D—— didn't need reasons. Of course he didn't do it merely out of spite. It was all about breaking down the ego, doubtless, and to ensure the People would be One. Then too, when D—— forced upon you something lesser, it increased the value of his own satiric love.

In Laurel's case, One wouldn't have called it punishment. D—— wasn't jealous of O——, not in that way. He was jealous of the piece of O—— he wanted for himself. D—— wouldn't have liked it if he'd known that either Laurel or I had deflected O—— from the ranch . . . and probably he did have his ways of knowing that.

So. Laurel had been back from Malibu for only a few hours when D—— looked at her piercingly: *I want you to go with Ned.* My blood jumped in me, but I didn't move. Laurel lowered her head and obeyed.

47

I was late to San Francisco because I got off the bus in Denver and started talking to a guy with jet-black hair and creamy skin and a cold spot in his eyes somewhere, that seemed to recede all the way through the back of his head. It drew me, that quality of the eyes, like I'd seen it somewhere long before, out there in the wine-dark emptiness of the universe where it came from. He'd whip his girls (there were four or five of us) high up on the backs of the legs where the marks wouldn't show, with a coat hanger or an extension cord. The marks showed anyway, a little, in the miniskirts and hot pants he made us wear. Besides the street he had a little call business, which seemed to specialize in rough trade.

So I learned something: there were ways I didn't want to be hurt. That wasn't my *bag,* as they put it back then. Did I know what was? In the end it wasn't hard to get away—he was lord and master of four square blocks but outside that territory he wouldn't have known where to go or what to do, so I didn't worry much about stealing his money. After all, he had stolen mine. The other girls were too limp to go with me, and I didn't trust them enough anyway. Maybe they'd been there too long, or maybe they liked what they were getting, or maybe it was the thin air up there in Denver, which did sometimes make it hard to think straight.

When I finally did arrive at the Haight, I learned something else: you can't make a living out of free love. It might be your bag, or it might not be your bag, but pretty soon my bag was empty. Not one bone to rub against another.

A woman has two purses.

Doing it with Louie was exciting at first because at the time, for a white chick who came from where I did, it was breaking a big important rule. But apart from that there was no real difference, or at least not a very interesting difference. Louie was full right up to his neck with ordinary mortal meanness, which worked well enough on the rest of his string, but didn't really do anything for me. In fact he reminded me of Ned in that way, except that I hadn't met Ned yet.

But despite his limitations Louie was kind of a cosmopolitan cat, who had no trouble stepping out of his turf in the Tenderloin. If I tried to lose myself in the Haight, he'd come find me. Once I went all the way to LA and he found me. And I by then knew there were ways I didn't like to be hurt.

When it came to the point, the answer was simple. I just hadn't known that I already knew. Louie made it easy for me, because when I touched the bayonet against his rib cage, he really didn't think I'd do it, didn't know I would until, for him, it was too late.

I'd learned the essence from my brother, long ago when I was small. You don't have to worry about resistance. Just keep pushing, and it goes right in.

48

I'll kill you if you tell, I said to Laurel, as we were coming out of Ned's cave that time, but I didn't mean it in an ugly or threatening way—it was more as if I'd said to her, *I love you.*

And Laurel seemed to take it as I'd meant it. As she came up blinking into the stark daylight, she swept back her hair and lifted her chin and gave me her most winsome smile. She said, "But you just told me I can never die."

49

I don't know fear, but I began to feel . . . uneasy. A new sensation, or one I'd not felt for a very long time. As if something were watching me, like prey.

I began to need the rifle with me always. Or as close to me as was feasible, which was often not quite close enough for comfort. Aside from the Pauley-related issues with this particular weapon, it was chancier now to travel with any sort of gun. Since the towers had come down in New York, there was endless trouble and shit about terrorism, and that not only in the east.

As if they really knew what terror was.

I couldn't take the rifle into work, of course, but I did have it stashed in the trunk of my car, whenever I left the trailer park. At night I took it into my bed and caressed it there, receiving the cold bright taste of metal on my tongue.

I missed the knives I used to own, the steel blade and the stone one. A gun, by comparison, lacked intimacy. But I had lost the knives I once had claimed, cast them away, despite their numinosity. Where did they go?

Sometimes by night there came the wash and clatter

of helicopter blades, circling over the rim where the town met the desert. In the silence after the chopper was gone, I felt the pressure of regard more keenly. Even through the trailer's flimsy roof. The eye of some invisible raptor high above.

50

I couldn't touch Laurel when she came back from her excursion with Ned. I couldn't reach her in any way. She had been raped before, one time or several. I knew it, though I'm not sure how I knew. Her eyes were blank. She lay curled in a ball. She didn't want me or anyone else to lay a finger on her.

D—— knew. D—— witnessed the depth to which she was cast down, and I think that may have been part of the reason he asked both of us to go to the canyon that night—not only because he knew what we could do. He wanted to give her something to get her over it, get her past the harm that he had caused her.

But I had already done my part, to help her rise above it. My part, which was probably also his. Where else after all could the voice have come from? The One voice that spoke to me louder now and at greater length and in more detail than was usual. That told me what I must convey to Laurel.

How nothing of such mortal nature could touch either one of us anymore—not where we lived forever.

Because we were One with the mask of D—— we had only to know our immortality. *Zoë*—the great wheel of our exit and return. All of these powers were already ours, if we but knew it. We had only to seal our knowledge with a sacrifice.

51

Now when I went out through the tear in the fence it was always too bright, no matter how far I walked toward the distance, like a spider creeping desperately across the fluorescent linoleum floor. Rattle of blades and a bald eye revolving somewhere overhead . . .

Already I knew, it was all starting to come down.

Again. It's . . . again.

Sometimes I longed for darkness of eternal night, and not this wasted pallor of the desert.

52

As I've said, he was a disposable person, and he didn't need much in the way of persuasion. I let Laurel do the craft of it: a sly smile and a switch of her hip, lure and allure to draw him in.

We took him to Ned's cave on the hill, so Ned would have to clean up after. I knew there would be nothing he'd dare say.

The striped djellaba spread beneath us. A shadow of padding and a wriggle of color on the stone floor of the cave. He understood that I was strangling him to increase his pleasure, and made no objection to it. A macramé belt, I think I used, and it might even have been his.

I wasn't prepared for Laurel's fervor. With every throbbing ounce of him squeezed down from his neck and into her. The whole of his life and death thrust into her.

OhmyGod, Laurel said. *O. My. God.*

At the very last moment she slipped away from him, deft as a weasel. The kris moved like water. It was as if I didn't know where it was coming from. Such an unimaginable ejaculation—blood and milk.

53

On my break I went to the fake diner and drank a neat whiskey and ate a slab of bloody meat. Tammy as always averted her eye from my plate. Then, as if she'd just suddenly remembered something—

"Did Marvin find you?"

"Find me for what?" I didn't get it. Marvin could have found me anytime in the last three hours, since I'd been right where he knew I always was, tucked into the green felt horseshoe of my table.

Tammy's eyes wouldn't stick on my face. She'd been a little shifty around me for a few days; I hadn't troubled to wonder why. She tucked up a strand of her watery red hair, glanced over at the television, which was prattling about homeland security, I think.

"There was somebody . . ." Tammy mumbled.

"What kind of somebody?"

Tammy shook her head, not looking at me. The poker games under the glass countertop played red and blue flashes across the papery skin that had begun to sag a little at the corners of her mouth. The clump of meat I had swallowed fell leaden to the bottom of my gut.

"Tammy," I said.

"I don't know," she said, her head wobbling almost like she had some kind of tremor. "I didn't really see him. I didn't talk to him. He talked to Marvin."

And lo, Marvin was waiting for me when I headed back toward the pit. As if he wanted to tell me something but then again he didn't.

"What?" I said.

"Guy looking for—somebody named Mae."

"A guy."

"A cop, maybe." Marvin's eyes were as slippery as Tammy's tonight.

"With a badge and a gun?" Look at me, Marvin.

"No." Marvin shrugged. "It wasn't like that." He looked toward the door. "Just a regular suit. But the shoes. He had cop shoes."

FBI. I knew. I'd known it was coming.

"He was looking for Mae Chorea," Marvin said.

"It's *Cho*rea," I told him. "Not Korea." Thinking—*I shouldn't have said that.* That wasn't the name on my light bill or my lease or my job application. I'd been living under the false name for so long that it had more weight than the real one.

"I didn't tell him anything," Marvin said. "It's not you, is it?" Now he looked at me, hard.

"Oh no," I said, and forced a smile. "Not me."

I had to go back to my table then, though I felt like somebody had dumped a bucket of spiders down the back of my neck. Wait and keep dealing, until Marvin wandered out of the pit. Then I made some excuse and closed my table. I had only a couple of marks on the stools, none of them a regular.

Must act normal normal normal as I carried my chips to the cage to turn in. Eye in the sky boring down on the tippy-top of my skull. But it didn't matter, what did it matter? Maybe a couple of eyebrows raised as I walked out.

On the steps I felt a moment of false relief, as the pale neon colors washed over me, touch of a soft dry breeze on my face, below and beyond the darkness of the desert. That Indian was coming up the steps as I went down, the one with the black hat and all the silver and turquoise accessories. Our eyes met, held each other for a moment as we passed. He seemed to look at me with pity, with compassion, even. *Why,* I thought, *why me?* Why would he look at me that way, himself a dying avatar of his exterminated race?

54

And of course from the first moment Marvin spoke to me I knew—I had already known what happened, how it must have happened. Who had made it happen.

Reach out and touch someone. Ping. Ping.

I wanted to be near her instantly, without the least delay. But it wouldn't be as simple as that, I realized. With all the heat about terrorism it would be the next thing to impossible—or no, impossible outright—to get a firearm onto a plane.

55

Then they finally found Eerie, dead in that motel. Just one more luckless mortal going back to shapeless clay— no reason that it should especially matter, yet each event has weight enough that when it falls it tumbles some other happenstance down with it. And yes, as D—— kept saying, it was all going to come down.

This time when Eerie died she died forever—no lover could lead her out a second time, away from the black throne. She'd tasted the food of death one time too many. Along with the overdose, she also appeared to have a broken neck, so One knew that Ned was probably involved, though no One said so—not within the People, and certainly not to all the cops who kept dropping by for the next few days.

I seem to see O—— in my mind's eye, lifting and cradling that sack of bones and carrion, wailing and gnashing his teeth as he carried the carcass of his lover toward the high rock in the dry hills. Singing a song that had no words, only screaming. But that can't be, because the coroner had surely hauled Eerie's body off to the morgue before O—— reappeared at the ranch.

His golden skin was drained now, to the color of old ivory, the color of dead bone. And now D—— had the hold on him that D—— had been wanting for so long. At long last, O—— had become One.

◦ ◦ ◦

Above the dry hills the air turned white—that shimmering electric pallor that pretended to promise rain in the desert, and the hard wind swirling up grit from the ground, while Ned climbed trees to nail up speakers behind D——'s speaking stone, and Crunchy and Creamy stirred up batches of gangster acid, cut with speed, with Tab or Mountain Dew in plastic garbage cans, so that it rained snakes instead of water, and I—I tore my robe to bare one breast and caught such a snake, its diamond back writhing over my hand, meaning to bind it around my brow as a living coronet, wedge head erect and spitting venom while I danced outside the borders of any mortal consciousness, whirling my thyrsus in one hand and a wildcat's spotted cub in another.

But I saw Laurel looking at me pale with shock or maybe fear—though her own head was a Medusa's now, festooned with bay enough to poison the whole company if someone brewed it up in one of Creamy's cauldrons. So then I flung the serpent from me, and when it struck a tree it turned to vine.

It seemed to me a cry of wonder roared up from the People then, and people rushed upon the grapes that burgeoned instantly, crowding and tearing their clothes on the bark, and using their own red-stained teeth as a winepress. And over it all arched the voice of O——...

· · ·

More and more people were coming in then, although not all, not even most of them, were One, but they came and came just because it was happening, a *happening* in the parlance of that time, and the thing that was occurring was O——. The album *Western Wind* had been released, so that O——'s bright visage was replicated hundreds of times in the plate glass windows of thousands of stores (along with that small cornered image of Laurel's higgledy-piggledy foot, which no one but I might ever recognize, and not for a long time) and O——'s voice flourished from the radio whenever anybody turned it on, but O—— wasn't doing live shows in the places he'd promised but instead was singing only to D——'s People, and it was for that people came and kept coming. Also there were rumors of free drugs.

There was such an avalanche of new people as to wash away the stain of Eerie's maybe-not-altogether-accidental death, which looked at first like a vexatious problem, the kind of thing that might not go away. One might have suspected in those early days a flicker of uncertainty around the mask of D——'s composure. Laurel had come back from her vagabond moment with O—— in Malibu, a little while before they found the body—dead for quite some time by then. Perhaps it wasn't wholly a coincidence that D—— had sent Laurel off to the cave with Ned while all the cops were first coming around, so the cops never did get to have a real deep talk with Ned, not until a good while later, when a whole lot more of it had come down.

Then O———'s voice came booming out of the speakers swung up in the trees, and more people swarmed in than the cops could keep track of, so the cops withdrew, though some of them still observed from the perimeter, bracing binoculars on the roofs of their squad cars, parked on the shoulders of the road. "Let them," D——— cackled, capering behind O——— on the crown of the rock they now used for a stage—"Let them lift up their eyes unto the hills!"

And O——— would transmute that into something more melodious.

Like iron filings courted along by a magnet, the People gathered below the rock. They had guitars up there, both of them, but mostly now it was O——— who transmitted D———'s words in song. These were the songs that ended up on the *Black Album*. How cold the coins that were laid on Eerie's eyes, we heard, how wide and deep and dark the Styx. But that was only the beginning, for many, many, must cross over. Every phrase full of the black and glittering beauty of death.

Fear coiled through the People, like a glossy blind black snake. One didn't cringe away from fear. D——— had taught us to embrace it. Fear was the very name of action. Fear brought our great deeds to bear. D——— told

us fear itself would be our Savior! . . . or it was O——
who sang it.

O——'s head a mere receiver for D——'s thought.
His diamond throat gave voice to D——'s words. If
either words or thought had ever properly belonged to
D——. They climbed the rock together, or no, as a single entity, Jesus, Jehovah, and Satan all rolled up into
One. Though afterward those words seemed pale and
rather flimsy; it was hard to believe they'd brought down
all they had.

I stood in reach of Laurel's hand, although I didn't
reach for it. There was no need. The black fear snake
curled tight through both our bodies, binding us
together. The voice from the rock above had filled our
skulls to bursting. All the People moved as One, the
Beast of Armageddon. One's answer boiled up from
dark mouth-holes like the crackle of flames in a great
conflagration. That One great voice drowned out those
fleeting voices I'd used to hear calling to me from time to
time, or maybe they had always been the same voice,
joined now in a single flooding stream.

* * *

When those congregations ended the men seemed
weary and somewhat abashed; they would limp away
toward the shelter of the buildings, but the women, boiling with dark energy, ran through the dusk into the bald
hills, still singing those songs till the sense fell out of
them and there was nothing left but a wordless ululation.

Sometimes, and maybe because we were tripping, those desert spaces broke out in lush foliage, so that we seemed to crash our wild way through a wet, vinous, fecund jungle, and finally Laurel and I always outdistanced the others. Her bare heels and mine pounding like a twinned heartbeat as we raced each other, each hunter and prey at the same time, across the stream that ran down from the falls, past the hooded opening of Ned's cave on the bare stony hillside, till we stopped breathless on the eastern ridge above the highway, Laurel's breast heaving, tatters of bay leaf still clinging in the snakes of her hair, and what I must have looked like I don't know.

Miles below, we could still hear the voices of the others winding through the arroyos, now falling away and now rising in pitch, like the howling of the hounds of Actaeon as they closed in on their master, whom Artemis had turned into a stag. Laurel and I were above all that, and yet somehow still awash in the stream of it, shining on each other waiting for moonrise, expecting to see the moon crowned with blood.

On other nights there was no moon. Cities and towns were all far distant, could not yet have stained the whole dome of the sky with the diffusion of their squandered light. Moonless, the color of night was a rich velvet black, as though we were submerged in chocolate, or a dark stream of blood in a deep vein.

56

I found a strange car on my street when I cruised into the trailer park. Ford Taurus, looked brand-spanking-new. Perhaps a rental. It was parked in my usual spot, and it looked empty when I passed it and drove on.

Lights were on in the trailer too. In a different configuration, I thought, than I had left them. But I use timers, and sometimes I change the pattern of the timers. A good deterrent, the local police tell us, next best thing to a dog.

A quarter mile outside the trailer park gate I aimed my car across the shoulder and cut the engine as it bumped over the low berm. I let it roll to a stop among the snarls of mesquite and creosote. A car passed by one way, then the other. Neither vehicle reached mine with its head-lights.

They must already have my car, I thought. Make and model, tag number, distinctive dents and everything.

Trying my very best to be quiet, I didn't get the trunk quite shut. Didn't want to slam it. I'd have to take care of that, if ever I did get back to this car.

Then I moved back around the perimeter, keeping

about twenty yards out from the wire. The steel diamonds gleamed erratically, catching stray shards of light
from trailer windows or from vehicles traveling inside
the park.

I moved in slow fits and starts, like an animal foraging,
or that's what I hoped. Or nothing, I hoped to appear as
nothing, black smoke dissipating over the plain. I wore
black jacket, trousers, white shirt, and a string tie. Faux
formal wear for the casino. The black must leap out
from the pale floor of the desert, but that's if anyone
were looking for something, and if they were they'd be
looking out of a well-lit area into a dark one.

Presently I had come to the rear of my own trailer,
and I could see the agent moving about inside. Yes, he'd
turned on more lights than I had on timers. All of them,
actually. Stumping around like he owned the place. I
seemed to be able to hear his footfalls ringing the flimsy
metal bell of the trailer.

Often as not they hunted in pairs. Were there two this
time? I saw only one. Searching, thoroughly but discreetly. If I returned after he had left I wouldn't find my
stuff dumped all over the floor or the cushions and mat-
tresses slashed open. No. He was leafing through every
book before replacing it where it had been. By the time
he was done he would have fingered all the containers in
my refrigerator, fondled every item in my clothes draw-
ers. Would he look into those albums of O——? No
reason he should find them particularly of interest. That

had never been reported as a crime. And yet—*reach out and touch someone*—there was a chance that he might know about it now.

And now he pushed open the glass sliding door and stepped out on the deck. He raised his head to sniff the air, considering. Square jaw lifting, pushing forward. He was tall, blocky, a faintly military profile. Light poplin jacket and his collar and tie undone. I was too far out and the light too dim to evaluate his shoes.

I saw his gaze begin to scan the desert. Eyes centered, he swept his whole head slowly, right to left. Then back again at the same slow rate. I was kneeling in the shadow of a stringy juniper, but he would certainly see me if I moved a hair. A flicker in his peripheral vision, to which he would return. He knew what he was doing, and so did I.

There was a fluttering in my throat. Could he see that?—no, of course not. Without moving my head I dropped my eye to the Starlite scope. It calmed me to see his image floating in that aqueous green circle, made him seem safely farther away.

Just one microscopic adjustment. Had he seen that?— or no, he was only lighting a cigarette. I think—

Pphhhhttt, said the silenced rifle. I probably shouldn't have done that, I thought. He'd gone down all at once without a whisper, like a marionette when you release the strings. When no one came to his assistance, I knew he must have been alone.

57

The slow molasses murmur of D——'s voice. Too low for Crunchy and Creamy to hear, where they sat on the pebbled concrete steps to the lodge, and yet they didn't need to hear it. Their heads came around in unison, and so did Stitch's head. Tuned, like roach antennae, to a single thought.

D—— then laid his cobalt eyes on me. The blue electricity flickering there. His hair looked soft. Womanly. Someone must have washed it recently. He was wearing his buckskins, I think, but not the moccasin boots.

"Find Laurel." D—— smiled, stroking his eyes across my body. I felt little hairs all over me unwillingly standing up.

"Take Laurel," D—— said. "Laurel should go too. It'll help get her, you know—"

Over it.

I lowered my head. Not in obeisance, but to keep our secret—mine and Laurel's. D—— was barefoot. Pale grimy toes spreading into the dirt.

I went to Laurel's room to get the Buck knife I'd been given, because I already seemed to know we would need throw-down knives for this excursion. It would be more than an ordinary slither. Laurel sat up from the tousled covers, raking the mess of her wild hair back, watching me heft the folded knife in my hand. Her green eyes coming alert as she woke.

"We're going out," I said, and slipped the knife in my ass pocket.

"D—— wants us both to go," I said.

Next we were all piled into the Fairlane. Creamy and Crunchy in front next to Ned, me and Laurel in the back. By the open back door, Stitch seemed to hesitate. Her back was to me, but I felt her give D—— an inquiring look. It was dusk, or past it, stars beginning to come out in the indigo sky, beyond the dry teeth of the mountains.

D—— shook his head and came to Stitch in a friendly manner. He curled a fingertip under the waistband of her pants.

"Write something when you're done," he said. "Stitch-Witch. You'll know what to say."

58

With the rifle case in the trunk of my car I had my handy
set of bolt cutters, and in my purse I had a box cutter,
which I'd carried there, for sentimental reasons, since
the day the planes flew into the towers. I could cut
myself a little with it sometimes, in dull moments and
discreetly, inside my upper arm or the concavity under
my hip bone.

Except for that I hadn't packed. I had cards in my
purse and a little cash. It hadn't seemed wise to go into
the trailer.

What would Pauley do? I thought confusedly, driving
south on 93. Back in the day I knew how to steal cars,
but twenty-first-century cars were too complicated.
Computer chips, alarms, all that.

I stopped at a roadhouse near I-40, pulling deep into a
big parking lot. Bass sounds throbbed from the windowless pillbox. Even money no one would come back soon.
I broke the tip of the box cutter twice, changing plates
with the car next to mine, but it didn't matter much since
I had plenty of spare blades.

59

It was just a day later when Pauley called. A night later, would be better to say. I'd thought it best to lay up during the daylight hours, tucking my car on the back side of a motel, where it couldn't be seen from the highway. At dusk I started out again. I was in Oklahoma or Kansas when the phone rang; it doesn't matter which. The same sleek black ribbon of asphalt unrolling endlessly before me in the dark.

"Mae . . ." Pauley's voice prickled in my ear. I felt a hint of pleasure, like being tickled by a kitten's whisker.

I made some sort of pleasant sound, and his voice hardened.

"What did you do?"

I didn't answer, but wheels were starting to turn in my head. What did he know? It had hardly been twenty-four hours. Well, a dead man would have been found outside my trailer. Almost certainly an officer of the law. And I, the *I* that worked at the casino and lived invisibly in the trailer park, had gone missing. And what did that add up to? And how did Pauley find out so fast? Of course, he was in the business of knowing things like that.

"Mae—" A tightness in his voice, getting tighter. "I thought you were just going to shoot snakes with that thing."

"He was a prowler." I probably shouldn't have said that. Pauley would know that I knew better. "You know, a peeping Tom."

"He was *fucking FBI*." The voice whined in my ear like a bee. I leaned on the gas and the car leaped forward. I was alone on the road out here and could see nothing but the two lines that defined my lane, rushing up in the cone of my headlights. So what? Was it all on the news already or did Pauley know through his special channels?

He was still there at the edge of my ear, but for a moment silent. I recalled how if I didn't hear from Pauley in a while I tended to assume he was dead. That could easily happen in his line of work. So when I did hear from him it was like—my mind started skating. Highway hypnosis, maybe. What if all the dead mortals started coming back to life? What kind of end would there be to it?

"You know that gun was hot already," Pauley said.

Well, yes. I did know that. Not that we'd ever discussed it.

"Where is that gun, Mae?" Pauley's voice had got quiet, almost seductive. "Have you got it with you now?"

I plucked the phone away from my head and looked at the little glowing screen. I thought of throwing it out the window, but that was unnecessary—the phone wouldn't tell him where I was or where I was going.

I thought of the smell of death on his hands. Imperceptible to others, to anyone but me. A little secret we had between us. That perception made me go with him, the first time.

"Don't worry about the gun, Pauley," I said. "I'm taking very good care of your gun."

For a minute I heard only the rush of my tires and the pull of night air against a weak gasket on the driver-side window.

"I don't know you," Pauley said, and then his voice was gone.

60

When it was finished and we left the house we stopped somewhere, nowhere nearby, because we saw a hosepipe in a yard. Ned held it high above us like a shower, then he turned it on himself, and next he started washing the bloody handprints off the white panels of the car, but that was when some guy came out of the house next door and scared us off.

So then we were back in the car, Ned driving. I don't know where we were—a neighborhood with streetlights. I thought probably he hadn't had time to get the car completely clean, and then there were other things that had to be done, I thought in a dazed, exhausted way—get rid of the bloody clothes and the knives.

Laurel slumped against me, her breath coming in gasping pants, like running or sex, some strenuous effort. I wished the sound of it would stop, and I wished Creamy would stop whining about how she'd bruised her hand. I'd bruised mine too. I think we all had. The stupid Buck knives had no hilt so when you stabbed and stabbed and stabbed in frenzy, the edge of your palm kept bashing against bone.

Streetlights strobed over the inside of the car, a pulsing brightness. In the regular flashes of light I saw my
hurt hand lying on my knee like a dead bird. I wasn't
sorry for anything but I remember feeling sorry for the
hand, as if it were no longer a part of me. As if it hadn't
done anything, but something had happened to it.

61

I did throw the phone out the window after all, because I suddenly felt I must repel it, like it had some kind of spy widget inside, a beacon that would draw my enemies to me. I was all alone on the highway, and I yanked the car into a bootleg turn, and fetched up on the grassy median, facing the way I had come. The phone screen still glowed on the roadbed, about a hundred yards behind.

I unpacked the rifle from the trunk, sighted with my elbows propped on the car roof. That sneezing sound. With a tiny pop, the light of the phone screen disappeared.

Reach out and touch that if you can.

A lone car passed on the other roadway, the suck of dark air and the headlight cone dragging away off to the west.

No, I thought, to Pauley, or whoever, or to nobody. *You don't know me.*

The car seemed undamaged, despite the brusque handling. I swung it back onto the road and drove on.

62

Sometime after it all came down, after the raid on the ranch, when D—— and the others were hauled off to jail—I went back to my brother.

Chillicothe, up on the Scioto River, had been a Shawnee town a couple of hundred years before. Daniel Boone had been a captive there, as I knew from Terrell. Maybe that was why he'd moved there. Or because he had a job, in the paper mill or the dog-food factory, something. Or because he couldn't be home anymore after he came back from Laos and Cambodia and Nam.

I couldn't go home either, and I had to go somewhere. You wouldn't say they were especially glad to see me. Mary-Alice was busy with her spawn, two of them by that time. My niece and nephew—what were their names? Billy and Bobbi. Bobbi was the girl—they spelled it with the *i*. They crawled around the TV room like fat and slightly sticky caterpillars.

And then the trial was on TV. Or not, because cameras were still forbidden in courtrooms, so there were only sketches. There was film of the girls on the corner outside the courthouse, but of course they couldn't have been Creamy and Crunchy and Stitch at all, because those three were inside, on trial with D——. It was another handful of girls who looked and behaved exactly like them, resembling one another completely, as insect larvae do.

Terrell, naturally, liked the story, and Mary-Alice hated it but she kept watching it all the time anyway, like a bird hypnotized by a snake. We would all watch it in the evenings, eating TV dinners off trays. Of course I never said anything, how could I? But I did wish they knew.

* * *

I'll kill you if you tell.

* * *

The war had finished Terrell, by which I mean it had perfected him. He'd come home with a string of shriveled ears he kept inside the closet door where you're supposed to hang your ties. Two Purple Hearts and a hard drug habit. So a lot of the time when he wasn't at work, he'd be driving off to Columbus or Dayton to score. Or he'd shut himself up with Mary-Alice and have me watch the children. Take them out of the house somewhere. There was a shabby little park.

Shawnee Chillicothe was never the same place the town is now. Chillicothe was wherever the clan leader lived, so it floated around all the time, like a dark dream. The Shawnee women would blacken their captives with ash before they killed them, burn and impale them on stakes before they killed them. They would skin small patches of the captives' arms or legs to see how well the captives bore the pain. Or maybe they didn't do such things at all and Terrell only said they did them.

Eventually I went back west. Partway back west. I couldn't stay there. Not only because they didn't want me to. I saw that it could never be the way it was. As for the children, they were only children, and Mary-Alice acquiesced in a different way than I had done. Where I'd learned to rush toward pain like a shark, she only whimpered haplessly beneath it.

A victim. She had made herself a victim. Terrell didn't want a partner anymore.

63

I wove the wreath of bay for Laurel, and set it on the cinnamon crown of her hair. The green of the leaves was fresh and luminous at first, then slowly dried to brittle gray in the parching heat of the desert. Those days she seemed to wear little else: the wreath, a shift; she walked barefoot till her heels parched too, and cracked and bled and dried again without her noticing.

All One had wine and smoke and song and screaming. There was not only the dry floor of the desert, caked with blood. In secret seams where water flowed beneath the falls there were tall trees, and grass and sometimes a few pale musky night-blooming flowers; Laurel knew those places and she knew where to find thick ropes of ancient grapevine hanging from the trees. Nights when we outran the hounds of Actaeon we might sometimes end up there, swinging in the loops of old vine *hairy as a monkey's tail,* as Laurel said, amidst the silver ringing of her laughter. Pumping in tandem, opposite, equal, so that Laurel rushed forward as I flew back. And once through a little tear in time I looked into my half-human childhood where the girl I'd been rocked on a tube-metal swing set screwed into the ground halfway between the house and garage, the movement soothing her, numbing her, washing her mind clean till nothing mattered, nothing at all, and she not even aware of the black empty eye of the garage attic window or the fountains of kudzu around and above her, smothering, strangling down the trees.

But with Laurel it was different, gladder and more powerful, for we could swing ourselves from giddiness through trance to ἑκσταση, flung upward to the sharp steel sickle of the moon with one star floating between its horns.

Eoui!

There, the voice of D——'s devoted women, running the pale floor of the night desert, their fierce cry now receding, now coming near—or it was Laurel's voice twinned with mine and neither of us knowing the purpose of those syllables born out of our throats by their own independent vitality.

Eoui!

Eouiiiiiii!

A thrill like fear when we heard that shrieking, even if it was ourselves that sounded it. Or less fear than awe at a life everlasting, resurfacing as it dived through death, *zoë* in its eternal cycle of return.

Then silence, save the creaking of the vines, the rush of our excited breathing, the whistling of stars across the inky sky. A phrase that whispered itself in the form of a small white stone.

. . . *I am your love* . . .

D——'s thought, long since, had married the voices in my head, and in my head and Laurel's was now one and the same utterance, and still in spite of all in the very thickest part of those nights there was our strange tenderness for D——, as if in the end *he* was the one who would be torn from us, torn by us, meat from bone.

Blood spilled on the sand would spring back green and limber, and from its berries would flow wine.

64

I want to say that maybe none of what I am about to tell is true, but only a version I prefer to dull reality, in which my kin still live their lives: the mother and father and the two children no longer small, no longer children, still here in the same place where they settled and began, or maybe elsewhere, some other indistinguishable place, imperceptibly sinking into the banality of mortal existence like meat dissolving slowly in a stew. If so, I have blotted them out of my mind with a story, as you may blot the stars with the palm of your hand.

If so, there would have been no graves, or only the graves of strangers.

* * *

On the third night, or maybe the fourth, I drove across the river north of the town, pulled over, and looked back. A peaceful vista, I suppose. In the small hours of the morning the windows of the houses were dark. A few had eave lights burning, for fear of prowlers.

In the air, the heavy sour smell of paper mill pulp fermenting. Downriver, the factory sparkled and hummed, emitting a great cottony cloud of yellowish smoke, spreading, dissipating into the night sky.

Close your eyes and think of Shawnee town. But then that hadn't ever really been exactly here.

The cemetery was there in a bend of the river, whose muddy coils twisted away to the south. It was cold here, much colder than Nevada at this time of year, and I hadn't thought to buy real winter clothes.

I looked into the star-speckled sky, then again down into the graveyard, the gray stones like crooked rows of teeth. The chill persisted. I got back into the car, cranked up the heat, and crossed the river on another bridge, back toward the center of town. The names were what you would expect in a little town like Chillicothe. Bridge Street. Main Street. Terrell's house had been off Water Street, on a short little spine running back to the fence of a golf course that blocked the way to the river from downtown.

I idled past, then let the motor die. The house was nondescript, a little brick ranch. It appeared to be inhabited now, though for a long time afterward no one had wanted to live there. In the starlight I could make out toys scattered on the patchy lawn, a soccer ball and a multicolored plastic tricycle. In a bedroom window was the glow of a night light and one of those round stickers that lets the fire department know there is a child inside.

◂ ◂ ◂

I read about it in the papers, and watched it replayed on TV. But I've forgotten most details, or else I never learned them. Suffice it to say that my brother's life ran off its rails of quotidian cruelty, its humdrum routine of domestic abuse, to bloom into something more spectacular, complete with the mother and children held hostage, the siege and rings of police with their weapons and bullhorns, negotiators bullying or pleading on the phone. Terrell had brought in gas cans to set the place on fire, but he didn't get a chance to light it. A SWAT team sharpshooter picked him off, but by then the others were already dead.

I was surprised, and not surprised, to learn that I had missed the rapture. It was as if I'd always known that he'd take everyone who mattered. All but me.

As for what went on inside, imagination fails me. What I did picture was the pyre that didn't burn. The house and whatever world it contained collapsing to its molten core. The hide and bone and tallow crackling, and the smoke of my brother's offering rising to the mottled sky.

But now the house was distinguished by nothing. It harbored other mortal lives.

I got back in the car and crossed the river. The cemetery was enclosed by a spear-pointed iron fence. The gates had been locked with a chain since my last visit. I broke it with the bolt cutters and went in.

The long grass crunched beneath my feet, white and

brittle with glittering frost. I hadn't been here in some time and it took me a while to find the spot. Let us suppose no sentiments were carved into the stones, only the dates and the four names. I'd dressed a way he would have liked, in a short skirt with no underwear, so I had only to stand and open my legs to piss all over his grave.

65

The car crept along the waterline, beside the great oily river of Babylon. In the bay, the goddess standing on her rock thrust her blunt metal torch into the sky.

Beyond, the glittering lights of the city. Packed close together, like jewels in a coffin. I saw two pillars of darkness where the towers had stood, fracturing slowly into the first light of the dawn.

Raze it. Raze it. Bring it all down.

As the sky paled and daylight grew, the black oiled surface of the river turned silver. There were waves from the wind, and a slow barge pushing through them. Wheel and scatter of gulls above the water.

The electric gleam died in the windows, and the thousands of buildings that remained turned their blind steely faces to the water and the wind. Along the opposite riverside I saw the tiny dark figures of mortals, scurrying on their errands, intent and insignificant as ants.

I reached toward the triumph of my own intention. *Daughter of Babylon, who shall be destroyed, happy is she who dashes your little ones against the stones.*

Silence.

The ragged hum of my own engine. Within the city opposite, there was a whistle, a squeal and a clatter as a thirty-story crane swung into action.

I steered the car into the sounding hollow of the tunnel, thinking bitterly, whatever is razed down is bound again to be raised up.

66

In the outer room of Laurel's office a secretary intercepted me. Did I have an appointment? No. My name? I invented something. Will she know what this is in reference to? No comment.

I composed myself to wait. Not long. The classroom clock over the inner door lintel advanced in little jits. A bell rang somewhere. There was the sound of young voices and hurrying feet. Then the inner door opened and Laurel leaned out, both her hands grasping the sides of the frame. Her green eyes were unfocused at first, then came clear.

"Come in," she said, with a half smile. It pleased me that she wasn't afraid. She had seemed surprised for only an instant.

Inside was an ornate desk, a grandfather clock, and, grouped around a small Persian rug, a coffee table and three upholstered chairs. Laurel pointed me to one of these and sat down in another.

"My predecessor," she said with a shrug, when she saw me looking at the furnishings. The little school was rich and Laurel worked in development, raising more money. It seemed an odd vocation for her, but probably she'd have felt the same about mine.

It seemed to me a wave went through her now and then, and that she weakened and bowed beneath it. Nothing so obvious, just a faint slackening of her body, the eyes going drifty. Anyone looking in on us might think, two well-preserved women, meeting after . . . perhaps we'd have a cup of tea.

"Coffee," Laurel called to the anteroom. The secretary brought it in with a stiff smile. We sipped. I went on looking at Laurel. She did seem softer, blurrier than before, in her body. Her face had not changed so much as that. Her chin had lost some definition and there were lines at the corners of her mouth and eyes, from her laughter and her smiles. Her cinnamon hair was lush and shining.

"It's the radiation," Laurel said.

"What?"

"The hair." Laurel picked up a lock to show me. "It comes back better after the radiation. For what it's worth."

I remembered how, back in the day, she used to follow my eyes to a target and see whatever I looked at with me. That wave came over her. Where was she?

"Sorry," Laurel said. "It's the drugs."

"You narced on me," I said. That antique term. Probably the one word had suggested the other.

"Did I," Laurel said. With an absent smile she set her

cup down in its saucer. A frail white cup of Scandinavian china. I had a flicker of wonder that it wouldn't be better to look poor when you asked for money.

"Oh, Mae," she said, shaking her head. "I'm taking a lot of dope for the pain. They're nice, they cover for me here, but half the time I don't know where I am or what I'm doing." The slackness in her throat came taut when she raised her chin to me. "Or what I did."

"They cover for you?"

Laurel laughed. "I'm well liked. I've done them quite a bit of good, over the years. And it won't be long. The doctors all said I'd be dead by last month. I've got ovarian cancer, Mae. Not much anyone can do."

"You told me," I said. "On the phone."

Laurel bit her lip and released it. She'd ratted me out on the phone as well. She might or might not have been thinking about that just now. The drifting look in her eyes as she lowered them might have been some kind of resignation.

"I'm in a lot of pain," she said.

"Oh," I said. Who isn't. But the thought of her suffering commanded in me a degree of respect.

"Morphine." Laurel's head moved back and forth. "I hear things. See things that aren't there. Sometimes I wonder if you ever really called."

The voices of the gods, I thought, and wondered if she heard them still. Again.

"I'm here," I told her.

Laurel didn't answer that. I looked around and saw a picture on her desk. A young woman with long black hair in ringlets, deep dark eyes, ivory skin with a faint tinge of gold.

"My daughter," Laurel said. "Ariadne."

"Oh," I said. "How old is she?"

"Thirty-something," Laurel said, with a certain slyness to the joke.

My mind went spinning for a moment. I pulled myself together, studying Laurel, groping for the old hard edge under this strange softness that blanketed her now.

"So," I said. "She's beautiful. Takes my breath away."

Then Laurel drew up, and I felt her old spirit strong in her, like a snake standing up in her spine.

"You can't have her, Mae," she said.

"She's a mortal," I said. "Anyone can have her."

"Do you think I want to die this way?" Laurel's green eyes flashed, then faded. She shook her head slowly— disbelief or resignation. "If I had some other choice. Supposing that crazy thing you claim was true. If it ever had been."

I'll kill you if you tell, I thought.

Laurel raised her tired eyes to me. "I've got to work," she said. "Pretend to work. We can meet tonight." She named a bar.

So the interview was over. According to her. Well, let it be.

"I never meant to harm you, Mae." Laurel was shaking her head in that same sad rhythm, like the brass pendulum on her predecessor's clock. "I didn't know what I was doing. I never meant to harm anyone."

Can you be serious, I thought, though truly I did not know what to say.

"Mae." Laurel turned her full attention on me as I stood. "I knew you'd come."

67

That night the canyon filled with screaming, like floods of rain might fill a gorge—our own cries and the victims' blended, fused, till there was nothing but this tapestry of sound. Now and again the flash of an image: Stitch running down a woman who'd broken out of the house somehow, closing on her across the yard, with the knife hammed in her fist like a long bloody tooth and the singleness of purpose of a hunting animal.

But all these things came to me in fragments. The shutter revolved over my vision, opening, closing it, opening again. Somewhere nearby in the room I could hear Creamy gasping in exhausted passion, frustrated that her victim wouldn't die.

"Take me," I heard the woman say, who faced me, hanging in the rope. She had fought hard, for a long time, but now she would surrender. Her head bowed. We had been in the house for a long time by then. It was surprising how much blood could spill out of a person, through how many wounds, and she still fight, cry out and live.

She had raised her head to speak, and for a moment I

held her gaze, until her head flopped down again and I summoned frenzy to slam the knife into her a few more times, with my bruised hand and my sore arm.

It stays with me, her dying look—how finally, how absolutely she accepted Até, the suffering passed on to her through me.

Again the dark wing strokes across my sight and when it passes I see Laurel, crouched on her haunches, both hands streaming with blood, on her face a childishly rapt expression, with her fingertip writing higgledy-piggledy on the wall.

68

You can't have her, Mae, was what Laurel said, but I wanted—*eoui,* how I wanted this mortal child, though not as my lover, not as my meat.

To bring a new birth from gray feathered ash . . . from the shivering dust that the lightning blaze had made of a foolish mortal mother.

And it ought to be Laurel and I together, swinging the newborn in its basket wreathed in vines. The vine sprang up where blood fell on the sand, and the child was reborn from the vine.

69

I waited outside the school for most of the rest of the day. There was a pretty little park, with a brick terrace, green benches and rows of ginkgo trees with their frail silverish branches bare. Some of them had been decorated with tinsel and red balls.

It was Christmas, the Christmas season rather. On my approach I had managed not to notice it. As I withdrew, awareness forced itself upon me. The school hallways were full of cardboard elves and Santas. And flummery decorations filled the windows of most of the shops. Groups of gay men strolled by, chattering urgently, tricked out in scarlet and hunter's green. Women passed, with clutches of bright shiny shopping bags, like inverted bouquets of balloons.

At three, the students came out boiling, gleeful. Their winter holiday must have begun.

I waited, motionless in the deep cold. Now and then I cheered myself with a quick shallow slash of the box-cutter blade across my palm or the inside of my forearm. It was twilight by the time Laurel emerged. She hesitated on the white steps of her building, turned back to the doorway above, where another woman leaned over her, murmuring some words of concern. Laurel tossed her head, flashed her old insouciant smile. She snuggled a bloodred scarf around her neck as she came toward the park where I was sitting, pinning it in place with a little enamel Christmas tree. Her smile had lost its brilliance by the time she was near, and as she passed, without seeing me, it looked rather a sad little smile.

Or if she saw me, she gave no sign. But it was very dark by that time. I drifted in her wake, like a bit of blown ash. She didn't look back. The cinnamon hair flowed over the scarf as the heels of her soft brown ankle boots clopped along over brick and concrete.

Laurel lived one avenue over, on one of the charming little side streets of the Village. A four-story brick building, its windows warm with yellowish light. She already had her keys in her hand and went in quickly, with a hint of stumble and recovery on the sill, under a lintel featuring a stylized cement lion's head, festooned with the ivy that climbed the brick wall.

I could have pictured her apartment, well-appointed, cozy, and snug.

Instead I began to walk downtown. I didn't know the city so well but all roads led to the same place really, like water running toward a drain.

Below Canal Street there began to be obstructions. Some areas were barricaded, meant to be sealed off. But enforcement was thin, the barricades permeable.

Hey, lady, some uniform called to me once. *Hey, lady, you can't*—but I went on my way without turning once to look at him, and he was wise enough not to follow.

I knew I must be near from the smell. And in this region the buildings were deserted, temporarily sealed with plywood, draped with cautionary banners. The city's dead core. Three months after the event it seemed impossible that smoke should still be rising from the center of the ruins, and still I seemed to see it, breathe it in.

Again, again, I felt my heart rising. Singing like a blade slashed through the wind.

What stopped me were the relics left by mortals. They began to appear everywhere, dropped on the sidewalk, wired into storm fences, taped crooked to the plywood sheets that sealed the shattered doorways of this zone. Mortals had arranged these things in tribute to their lost ones: photographs and talismans, flowers and strings of beads.

Beneath these wayside shrines, small scented candles burned. I saw a shrouded woman come and light one and remain there crouched on the sidewalk for a moment, lowering her head. I thought of Laurel but it wasn't Laurel. Her head was completely wrapped in a fringed shawl.

When she departed, I approached—above the candle she had lit, a photo of a husky youth, strong jaw, white smiling teeth framed by a U-shaped mustache. Both his eyes and his nose were shining. He might have been a little drunk when the picture was taken. There was a note that said *I love you.* Many notes, strung along the fence wire with the photos. *I love you I will never forget you. You are forever alive in my heart.* Notes and medals and keepsakes and bunches of flowers withering in the winter wind.

I am your love, we had been told. And then—

O——'s love for Eerie brought her out of death, the first time, as my love for Laurel drove her deeper in. The way that O—— loved Eerie made it rain down water, and I loved Laurel so the rain was blood.

It was not unknown for a goddess to surrender immortality, reduce herself to the world of mere living, to share with a mortal lover everything—down to death and dissolution. But I couldn't recall, that night on the street, the name of a single one who had done so. And Laurel's mortal lover was long dead.

To weaken. To weaken oneself so.

Now and then a child's toy hung there among the other mementos. That put me in mind, somehow, of the plastic trike in what had been my brother's yard in Chillicothe. I drew the box-cutter blade across my palm to scrape that thought away.

70

Across the way from where Laurel lived there was another little park, filling a triangle of otherwise useless space where a street flowed into an avenue. A chest-high fence of iron spears surrounded it. The surface of the ground was sandy and there were other trees, bigger than ginkgos, but without their leaves I didn't know them.

I sat there, waiting in the dark.

I had bought a duffel bag for the rifle and my other gear, thinking it would be at least a little less conspicuous than the long hard case the rifle had come in. In fact I could open the bag at one end just enough to brace the tip of the barrel on an iron fence rail, and at the other focus the Starlite scope across the avenue and down the street to the doorway with the ivy-wreathed lion's head above it.

From somewhere I heard Christmas music. From a car—the sound dwindled as it passed. A pair of cops strolled by and didn't see me. Perhaps they saw a nonde-script middle-aged woman with a shapeless bag. Laurel had set our drinks date fairly late. I found her briefly in the scope as she came down her doorstep, the green fluorescent image swimming toward me in the glass. She was, I think, a little distracted, for she passed the park without seeing me, and went into the bar on the other side. I zipped up the duffel bag and followed her in.

"Oh," said Laurel, dimpling. "You're here."

She unwound her scarf and shrugged out of her winter coat. Beneath, to my surprise, she wore only a sleeveless red shell. She gave the sort of dramatic shiver that would make somebody want to put an arm around her, but we were sitting across a small square table from each other.

"Aren't you cold," Laurel said.

I shrugged.

"They have great burgers here," Laurel advised me.

She went to the bar and brought back a glass of neat bourbon for me, single malt Scotch for herself. When she sat down I looked at her bare upper arm for a sign of a scar. There might have been a couple of fine white lines; in the dim light it was hard to tell. Laurel's flesh had slackened a little, but in this kind of lighting she still looked good.

"They have a great jukebox," Laurel said, tossing back her glossy irradiated hair as she turned her head to look at it. "All the good old stuff."

The room warmed as we drank our whiskey, and as

more people began to come in. A younger crowd mostly but some near our age. To one of those good old songs on the jukebox there was a flicker of hesitant dancing.

We talked, somewhat haltingly. Laurel was stoned on her pain drugs, I realized; though she covered it reasonably well, it muffled her in a deep layer, below the warmth of the Scotch. She talked, somewhat wanderingly, of her days here before and after the planes hit the towers. How she happened to be nearby when they fell (some banal, coincidental reason). The shock, horror, grief, and dismay, gradually fading into simple inconvenience. One lived with it awkwardly, a dry, diminished thing.

In return I told her a few casino stories. A couple of them made her smile. Sometimes her hand seemed to tremble a bit as she raised her glass to her lips. Once without thinking I reached out with a tissue and blotted a droplet of Scotch from her chin. Our faces came very near, not touching.

And although nothing had been said we arranged another meeting, to say it again. Coffee, next morning. The coffee shop was two doors from the bar. It occurred to me that Laurel had contrived to pass most of her days in a space even smaller than the wretched provincial town I grew up in. We were only a couple of blocks from her school.

When she opened her wallet to pay our tab, a card fell out, without her noticing. I ducked under the table to retrieve it. A laminated photo, slightly smaller than a playing card. I hid it in the cup of my palm. Ariadne was younger in this one, in her early twenties, perhaps. Somebody had put one of O——'s old songs on the jukebox, but I didn't really need that cue—the resemblance was plain enough without it.

When, I was wondering. It couldn't have been her detour to Malibu, because there was too much time in between. She would have been showing and she wasn't. So it must have been the very last time we were all together.

I snapped the picture down on the black shellacked surface of the table. Laurel picked it up, with a faintly wistful expression, and filed it back into a slot of her wallet.

"I never loved him, you know," she said, with that same swimming, distant look. And she shook her head, or its own weight wagged it. "Nobody loved Orpheus— it was only the music. I loved you."

71

We came upon O—— wandering in the wilderness, strumming and singing sad songs of Eurydice, whom he had brought back from the realm of death, but who had returned to abide there forever . . . Or to be more exact it was we who were wandering, while Orpheus sat upon a stone, cross-legged with his honey-colored guitar in his lap, and snakes and horned toads and coyotes came out to hear him sing those mourning songs. Laurel and I joined the audience of beasts, looking like wild animals ourselves, no doubt, after days of hitchhiking and walking through the brush—and mostly we'd been afraid to hitchhike either, after the raid on the ranch.

O—— gave us some tabs of blotter acid, or it was we who gave it to him—I'm sure we were already tripping when we found him. Yes, Laurel had a whole sheet in her sandalwood box, decorated by an artist who'd laced all the tabs together with loops of vine and psychedelic blossoms, and in the center of each square the brooding yellow eye of an owl . . .

* * *

We didn't know the cops hadn't come about the murders. The raid was over some beef about stolen cars in the beginning, but nobody knew that when it started, and Laurel and I didn't find out until after the whole scene with O——— had gone down.

At the first sound of a siren, Laurel, quick as a cat, snatched up her box, dove out of the room and squirmed up under the ramshackle building. I couldn't process what had set off her alarm, but I snatched a string bag and followed her without thinking. D——— was the only other one of his People who had the time or thought of hiding. He folded himself up completely into a two-by-three cabinet under a sink in the lodge basement; a single strand of his hair hanging out gave him away. But we only learned that part from the news later.

City police and sheriffs had come together—a joint operation with dozens of badges. They were herding all the People out of the buildings and into a big anxious quarrelsome gaggle in the yard in front of the lodge. Huddled together under the floor, we could hear, could almost feel the jump boots thumping on the splintery boards above us.

Then a couple of fat flashlight beams began probing underneath. Down at the school-bus end and too far off to find us yet. It had gone quiet overhead. I elbowed Laurel and wriggled out, belly flat to the cooling sand. By luck it was a moonless night. We moved through it sheathed in that hot clinging darkness. When we reached the cover of some scrub we both sprang up and ran.

We went scuttling along, a few dozen yards from the highway shoulder, taking cover whenever a set of headlights appeared. Presently the whole caravan of police and sheriff's cars and paddy wagons came out of the ranch and motored past us, in the direction of downtown LA. An hour or so later we had reached a crossroads where there was a gas station and a little store. We straightened up, sighed, picked burrs from our hair.

"Shit," Laurel said, breaking her stride toward the lighted doorway and clawing at all her jeans pockets at once. She'd forgotten her wallet with the detour fund. Of course I never had any money. I looked in the bag I'd snatched as we ran: my two knives wrapped in a tie-dye T-shirt and that was all.

• • •

O—— had a room at the Joshua Tree Inn. Laurel and I got in the tub together. We were both so filthy the water turned gray and we had to drain it and start over again. We had left the door open, and once we were clean I began to sense Laurel's pique at O——'s lack of interest. He only kept singing the sad eerie songs.

She looped a towel around her hips and walked into

the bedroom with her heavy breasts swaying. O—— did not appear to notice her. His music went on. There was a bottle of tequila on the dresser. Laurel picked it up and swigged.

Then, I think, we all took another tab of acid.

✦ ✦ ✦

. . . and Laurel reached between his legs and brought his member to life with her hands, with her mouth, and yet he remained indifferent to her, even as she bestrode him, rocked into him—the singing continued. I'd taken a rawhide lace from his boot, but when I moved toward his throat from behind, Laurel shook her head and plucked it from my fingers. She reached for the small of my back and soon had arranged the three of us in a combination as dexterous as any D—— could have devised. Thus for some time we all moved together, our voices, mine and Laurel's, keening higher and higher into a crescendo of O——'s song, and yet O—— never seemed to know we were there—I don't think I'd have known I myself was there, if I hadn't caught sight of myself in the cracked mirror behind the bottle on the dresser, hips pumping mechanically, my face a black hole . . .

✦ ✦ ✦

. . . then afterward, Laurel roused herself from a daze— she had slipped down the coverlet to slump on the floor. On the edge of the bed, O—— had taken up his guitar again, and not for an instant had he ever stopped singing. Now that mirror captured his face too.

I saw her open the sandalwood box.

She stood, writhing her hips like Salome, the kris flickering in her hand, and spun on her heels, like a top, her limbs braiding and flowing together like water, as her blade opened a fine red line on her upper arm—and I was dancing myself by then, with Laurel, around O——, bayonet in hand, she and I laying soft cuts on each other and then upon O—— as his song went on—giving him deeper and deeper cuts, as he never seemed to feel any of them.

. . . tripping, the light from the bare bulb overhead seemed so beautiful, and all our movement was a poem. Laurel's blade struck into O—— like a snake and then as she twirled into her own center stroked another cut on her upper arm—a shallow one, though it wept ruby beads of blood. Laurel always knew how not to hurt herself too much.

* * *

. . . and I used the bayonet to break bone, but the stone knife lifted the beating heart from his ribs and we shared it between us, like a bowl. I never saw either of those knives after that, as if they had served their ultimate purpose, and of course I couldn't safely have gone back for them . . .

* * *

It finished elsewhere, deep in the desert, and yet there seemed to be a broad rushing river, streaming iridescent colors, like a peacock's tail. Above there swung a sickle moon, and we had hung his harp upon a willow, and we had torn him limb from limb, and I swear—I swear!—as it went down in the flood, his head still sang.

72

On the morning after, in the bleak daylight and the gritty, parching wind of the desert, we went our separate ways.

73

Love. The notion troubled me. The word. Since Laurel had last uttered it. Back in the day, it was all love this and love that and luvluvluv till the sense was all rubbed away from the sound and all that remained was a little squeak of nothingness. The last exhalation of a mouse as its spine popped in a trap. Though once upon a time it had meant something.

. . . I am your love . . .

That whisper kept plaguing me as I plied my bolt cutters in the effort to get into the place the television called Ground Zero—that is to say, those charnel pits where the towers had once been. The chains and padlocks were too heavy to cut, and finally I had to go through the links of the storm fence. In the process I dislodged more of the relics strung up along the wire. Down fell a photo, a note, a holy medal, and an origami crane. I followed, skidding on my heels, then finishing the slide on my tailbone.

Up rose the dust, a toxic silt. My nostrils thickened with the odor of death. So many deaths, hundreds upon hundreds. The smoke of the sacrifice rising on high.

Here it was very, very dark, and in my descent I had come to rest on one sore hip, holding up two claws full of dust. This whole zone of the city was blacked out still and the sky above the well where I lay was very far from clear.

Zero

o

o

I sifted the dust in my two hands and found in one what seemed to be a locket on a chain. The other held a jagged shard of bone. I pressed its point into the muscle of my palm and I began to hear a hum—

oooooooooooo

—a kind of ghostly screaming. Or maybe it was song. So many dead, the smoke of the burning fat twisting up between the horns of the altar:

o

o

A hole in the world. Anything could come through it.

I stroked the groove in the bone where the marrow had been, surprised at the sudden sharp pain in my heart. In Laurel's office I had remembered D——, not the shell of his carcass lying in bondage, but D—— in his transfigured form—and when we slew him as a child one of us held a mirror to his face, not only to distract him from the knives but also to catch and fix his soul for its next coming. Sure to come.

In the end they said that all we ever had was murder but there had been love too among the People.

o

what there had been

my love . . .

Even here was a little fugitive radiance and up above I could see a faint light catching on the storm-fence diamonds, brighter on the broken links where I had just now cut them, though down in the bottom of the well where I lay, there was the most absolute silky darkness, the color of night, unless it was some fault in my vision that I only saw it in monochrome. That ghostly singing rose, expanded—a crying wind. I clasped and unclasped the bone in one hand and in the other the locket popped open but it was too dark to see the picture and in any case the picture was reduced to the merest white feather of ash. How I missed the People after all, and to my dismayed surprise, I found that I missed other people too. Some whose names I'd long forgotten. Laurel most of all.

As if this perfect blackness had torn itself completely open, permitting me to see all of them, in all their spectral colors. How it must weaken me, this . . . *feeling*. As if mortality bore down upon me too. As if mortality could bear me down.

I thought with a still deeper dismay, *What if I can't do what I have come to do?*

There was not yet any sign of daylight, but somehow the armor of darkness was weakening. At a distance, the noise of a crane . . . If I stayed here much longer, I would be seen.

There in the corner I could see a way to climb out, and I moved toward it. My hands empty now, for I had lost the tokens that they'd held.

I wanted to lick the blood from my face, but it was only water.

74

Do you think I want to die this way?

Perhaps I hadn't thought it through. I sat in the iron-railed triangle park, alone except for two homeless men, heaped in their rags on two parallel benches, now and then stirring in their sleep. Beneath them, tatters of newsprint blew fitfully between the claw feet of the benches.

The light came up; it would be a clear day. Sunny. In the bare branches of these trees there was a twittering of I don't know what birds.

I had expected children, funneling out of the side streets toward the school. But their vacation had begun, so they would still be sleeping.

As for the other mortals, they pursued their errands in the most ordinary way.

The door below the vine-wreathed lion's head opened. Here she came, tightening the scarf around her shoulders and her neck. Quick confident steps advancing into the brightening day. In the ground glass of the rifle's scope, she looked almost an abstract figure. Crosshairs settling on the hollow of her throat.

She saw me then, and her chin lifted. Her eyes and her whole face lifting and lightening as she hurried to our meeting.

Her life at my fingertip, one more time.

I have no other story to tell but this one.

ALSO BY MADISON SMARTT BELL

ALL SOULS' RISING

In this first installment of his epic Haitian trilogy, Madison Smartt Bell brings to life a decisive moment in the history of race, class, and colonialism. The slave uprising in Haiti was a momentous contribution to the tide of revolution that swept over the Western world at the end of the 1700s. A brutal rebellion that strove to overturn a vicious system of slavery, the uprising transformed Haiti from a European colony into the world's first Black republic. From the center of this horrific maelstrom, the heroic figure of Toussaint Louverture emerges as the man who would take the merciless fires of violence and vengeance and forge a revolutionary war fueled by liberty and equality.

Fiction/978-1-4000-7653-6

MASTER OF THE CROSSROADS

Master of the Crossroads delivers a stunning portrayal of Toussaint Louverture and his struggle against the European powers to free his people in the only successful slave revolution in history. At the outset, Toussaint is a second-tier general in the Spanish army, which is supporting the rebel slaves' fight against the French. But when he is betrayed by his former allies and the commanders of the Spanish army, he reunites his army with the French, wresting vital territories and manpower from Spanish control. With his army one among several coalitions, Toussaint rises as the ultimate victor to take control of the French colony and establish a new constitution.

Fiction/978-1-4000-7838-7

THE STONE THAT THE BUILDER REFUSED

The Stone That the Builder Refused is the final volume of Madison Smartt Bell's masterful trilogy about the Haitian Revolution. The trilogy "must be considered among the most important artistic accomplishments of our . . . century [and] could easily cement Bell's reputation as one of his generation's greatest authors" (Harold Bloom). "[It] will make an indelible mark on literary history—one worthy of occupying the same shelf as Tolstoy's *War and Peace*" (*The Baltimore Sun*).

Fiction/978-1-4000-7618-5

TOUSSAINT LOUVERTURE

At the end of the 1700s, French Saint Domingue was the richest and most brutal colony in the Western Hemisphere. A mere twelve years later, however, Haitian rebels had defeated the Spanish, British, and French and declared independence after the first—and only—successful slave revolt in history. Much of the success of the revolution must be credited to one man, Toussaint Louverture, a figure about whom surprisingly little is known. In this fascinating biography, Bell combines a novelist's passion with a deep knowledge of the historical milieu that produced the man labeled a saint, a martyr, or a clever opportunist who instigated one of the most violent events in modern history. The first biography in English in over sixty years of the man who led the Haitian Revolution, this is an engaging reexamination of the controversial, paradoxical leader.

Biography/978-1-4000-7935-3

DEVIL'S DREAM

With the same eloquence and grasp of history that marked his award-winning fictional trilogy of the Haitian Revolution, Madison Smartt Bell turns his gaze to Nathan Bedford Forrest, the most celebrated and reviled general of the American Civil War. Here we see Forrest on and off the battlefield; we see him treating his slaves humanely even as he fights to ensure their continued enslavement; we see his knack for keeping his enemy unsettled, his instinct for the unexpected, and his relentless stamina. As *Devil's Dream* moves back and forth in time, a vivid portrait comes into focus: a rough, fierce man with a life full of contradictions.

Fiction/978-0-307-27991-0